BOULLI BEEF

BOULLI BEEF

Mr. DH

Library of Congress Control Number:		2013923152
ISBN:	Hardcover	978-1-4931-7739-4
	Softcover	978-1-4931-7740-0
	eBook	978-1-4931-7738-7

This is a work of fiction. Names, characters, places and incidents either are the
product of the author's imagination or are used fictitiously, and any resemblance
to any actual persons, living or dead, events, or locales is entirely coincidental.

This book was printed in the United States of America.

Rev. date: 03/24/2014

To order additional copies of this book, contact:
Xlibris LLC
1-888-795-4274
www.Xlibris.com
Orders@Xlibris.com
551582

To write, one needs to believe, to be creative, one needs passion; to live, one needs love.

To that one special lady that brought all of these together that ignited a fire in my soul and heart. Colleen, I write for you.

Mr. DH

INTRODUCTION

This novel is fictitious. The characters and incidents that are mentioned never really happened, and if they did, it's purely coincidental. In writing, I changed the names of certain prominent persons to bring continuity to the story (particularly in referring to persons that were actually involved in the Boer war. This was done to protect them.)

The Second Boer War was one of the most expensive wars Britain ever fought. It was a ghastly war with many firsts: the trench warfare introduced by the Boer armies and concentration camps introduced by Britain under Lord Roberts, which will always be a very dark period for Britain. Although certain people like Emily Hobouse tried to bring the atrocity to the British people's attention, she never succeeded.

There are stark memorials all over South Africa of the thousands of woman, old people, and kids that died in these camps. The world doesn't know or care to know what had happen. Many all over the world have asked for apologies for similar atrocities that were done by other nations, but to my knowledge, Britain has never apologized for the demise of a whole generation in South Africa.

The real victims were the indigenous people of Africa. They were seen as savages and were treated as such and disposed of as commodities rather than people. Thousands of black people were also placed in camps with no sanitation, no food, and no water. They were basically just left there to die. They were the real true victims that got caught up in a war that had nothing to do with them.

In writing it was my intention to show that war and its aftermath lingers on in people for decades. The damage done to people's minds and souls never ever seemed to heal. For any individual to be totally free, they had to let go, get revenge, or forgive.

Revenge is a bitter thing as it never really sets one free. What sets one free is to break the bonds that have been placed on your being and decide within one self that you no longer want to be bound by hatred and fear. By using the characters in this story, I tried to show what could have happened to people after this war.

CHAPTER 1

The sun was liquid heat that shimmered and danced on the horizon like a dragon blowing flames on unprotected victims. Sweat couldn't form as it just burnt away before it could be seen. A man on the horse was riding like a demon.

His pursuers were very far behind.

Danny Venter looked back to see if he could spot any movement in the liquid heat that washed like water over the horizon. He had been at it for more than an hour; the horse was a ghostly white powdered gray as the salt crusted its hide.

"Did they give up? God, I hope they gave up. If they catch me, I am dead, that's for sure."

He was a Boer, Dutch for farmer.

He looked about realizing that they might have come to the conclusion that no one was going to survive out here without water. A barren landscape with small shrubs that was more brush than anything else—that's what this was. Called the Karoo, a dry arid piece of land to the north of the mountains that shielded Cape Town and locked in the rain and moisture. No water. Very few if any trees, just the lonely camel-thorn trees that seem to defy all odds and grow in this oven. This was bad, and he had doubts if making a run for it was such a good idea. If he did not find shade or water and quick, both he and the horse would die.

They caught him and several of his fellow Boers as they hoped to get into the Cape Province and destroy some rail tracks and attack some small British columns. A stupid mistake when crossing the Orange River in daytime had them caught. British soldiers were waiting for them as they came out the water. He longed for that same water right now.

The war was coming to an end; only a few generals were still evading capture. Most of the land in the Free State had been burnt and farms, destroyed cattle, killed, woman and children taken away and placed in concentration camps.

The British soldiers or Rooinecks, as they were called due to their sunburned necks, had been at war with the Boer republics for two years.

Standing in the saddle, he tried to see if there was any shelter from the heat anywhere, but just the flat hills and occasional thorn tree met his eyes. Maybe one of those trees, but then he would be seen for miles around. *Or maybe the hills would have a bit of an overhang with some shade*, he thought to himself.

The ground crunched as the horse slowly moved on. The hill in front of them was a little taller than most, but its sides showed no sign of any rock formation that would bring shade. Just the typical straight-up cliffs that formed a ring around a flat Plato top and a slanted sandy bottom, tapering off to the flatness of the barren landscape.

He looked back nervously, but there was nothing out here at all. No one would venture out here in the heat of midday in the summer.

As he skirted the hill, he saw some tracks that led to a small opening that led into the inside of the hill. He made his way toward this deep rift in the side of the hill. Barely wide enough for him and the horse, he dismounted and started in. The heat in this bowl was stifling thick molten air. The sides of the small crevasse was brown wind worn and looked like rust. Steep, a good seventy to eighty feet straight up. Tracks meant animals came here; if they did, there was a reason why this place, only one reason: water. As he rounded one of the small outcrops inside this small bowl, the horse reared up. "Slowly, boy, slowly." He was getting dizzy form the heat and wasn't sure what was real and what wasn't. He thought he saw some movement then again. He saw them, and there were a lot of them, puff adders all over trying to get out of the sun. They cowered in to the smallest shadows. These flat thick brown-scaled snakes could strike with a speed faster than lighting and with venom that would kill in minutes. He was about to back off when his eyes caught the small green patch under an overhang to his right. The overhang formed a cave about thirty feet into the side of the rocks. That meant only one thing: water.

With a broken branch from a thorn tree growing inside this heat bowl, he started flicking the snakes away that were too close for comfort. He started making a path to the green grass. Once there, he saw it—water. The pool was small, about three feet in diameter and about eight inches deep, but it was water. He drank, so did the horse.

The best water ever.

"We might still make it, buddy," he said to the horse.

Taking some of the water in his hat, he washed all the salt of the horse. The animal shivered when he did it.

He looked around. The snakes were slowly making their way back.

"Shit," he said.

Flicking some away again, he proceeded to clean a big area. It was obvious. If he wanted to stay here tonight, he would have to make a plan with the reptiles.

After drinking some more water, he started to build a low wall with some rocks and fill the gaps with some of the broken branches from the thorn tree that was laying about.

When he was done, he was tired and hungry. The horse was okay as it was feeding on the green vegetation next to the water. There wasn't much, but at least, it was something.

Danny had nothing with him. He undid his shoelaces and made a small trap, hoping to snag a "dassie" or hare. Dassies are small rodent-type animals that live on the rocks and hills all over this part of Africa.

Then he lay back and in no time fell asleep. When he woke up, the sun was just setting. The noise of the dassie in the snare was what woke him up. He realized once he caught it that he had no ways of making a fire or even skin it. Not having the energy to try and make a fire, he let the animal go.

While he sat there, he noticed something that twinkled near the rocks he just placed; he stood up to look.

Fortune shines on us all. For some many times, to others but once. How she smiles is never the same. How long she smiles is always different.

The diamond in his hand the size of a hen's egg. He swallowed hard shaking as he held the gem in his hand. He was about to place it in his pocket when he saw that there was more and more. The whole inside of the bowl was just one big mass of diamonds of any shape and size you could think of. There was even one as big as his fist.

He sat back and laughed.

The sun was just about down, and being in this bowl amongst all these snakes was not going to be fun. Taking his shoelace and making a bow, he found a nice piece of thorn-tree branch and started to see if he could get a fire going. It took long very long, and it was pitch dark when he saw the small ember in the wood. He blew gently and then placed some of the small dry grass on the ember praying that it would start up. It looked like it would then died; he started again, this time the ember was there quickly. He blew gently placing the grass on the ember. The flame was small then another, and then he had a small fire going. *Pity, I let that damn dassie go, could have just roasted him skin and all on the fire.*

The fire lit up the inside of the bowl in the hill. Everywhere he looked, he saw the twinkle of the diamonds. I am rich, he thought. Then it hit him, and he realized. If anybody knew, especially the Rooinecks, they would kill him and the find would go to them. No, he wouldn't take one stone with him. It was way too dangerous. If caught again and he had the stone, they would make him talk as to where he found it. No, he wouldn't take one.

Early the next day, he felt better and decided that he would wait one more day; then, he needed to get going. North find De Wit join up with him. He caught another dassie and cooked it. Then killed the fire as he was scared the smoke might give him away.

It was like being in a giant drum as the sound of the shot reverberated inside the bowl.

The bowl had one way in, the small little gap in the wall of the bowl like canyon that Danny had made his way into. Except for two very old thorn trees and the small patch of grass by the water, the bowl was barren. Some monolith-type formations were inside the bowl like sentries standing guard about five to six feet tall and about four feet in circumference.

Unlike the rest of the rocks on the outside of the hills, these rocks were blue—the blue of Kimberlite diamond bearing rocks. Even the shale on the base of the bowl was blue. The whole inside of the bowl was no more than sixty meters in circumference.

Danny fell backward his eyes darting around the inside of the bowl, but there was nothing there.

He quickly got to his feet and with stick in hand flicking the snakes out of the way. He made his way to the rim of the canyon to look and see who fired that shot. There was no one where he looked. Scurrying around just below the rim as best he could, avoiding the snakes till they came in to view—four soldiers and a black man. They had him sitting on his knees. They hit him, kicked him, and even urinated on him. Hog-tied, he could not defend himself.

Danny felt like running down there and beating the shit out of them. Not because of the man but because they were Rooinecks.

"I can't do a bloody thing. I have nothing to defend myself with. *Shit, shit, shit*, he mumbled to himself.

By late afternoon, they had started a fire, and one of them produced a bottle of brandy. It didn't take long with the heat for them to lay, passed out around the fire.

The black man lay lifeless to one side.

Take your horse and make your way out of here before they see you or wake up. He thought to himself.

He slowly made his way out the canyon, was about to move away when he saw the black man beaten and bruised eyes swollen shut.

He moved of a short distance, tied his horse to one of the shrubs, then made his way back. When he reached the black man, he placed his hand over his mouth. There was little resistance.

"Keep quiet," he whispered in his ear in Dutch. Then he untied him and took him to the horse and told him to him to wait. "Don't move even if you hear shots, okay?"

Heat and booze don't work well together and not only were these men out, but they were sunburned as well. First two guns then a knife, a water bottle, a sack of food, lots of ammunition, and two horses. That's what Danny found,

It was dark now, and the small flames from the fire and the moon were the only lights.

He gave the Blackman some water, told him to drink slowly.

"Wait here," Danny said again in Dutch.

"Yes, boss," the black man replied in Dutch.

Making his way to the opposite side of the soldiers, he first tied two cans to a spare horse's tail. He looked around in the moonlight; then he saw a big aardvark hole. *That will have to do.* He was thinking.

Taking the revolver, he had taken from one of them, he fired two shots in their direction, holding on to the horse that was baying and jumping about. Then he shouted something in what sounded like a black language.

Pandemonium broke out with the drunken and in a daze soldiers.

They were shouting blaming and pointing to where the black man had been tied up. Then he fired a second shot in their direction as the second shot went off, they scrambled for cover then looked in the direction of the shots, and in no time, they were off two per horse. The horse with the tins was running off like mad. This was what they were following; eventually, the cans would fall off, and no one would be the wiser. Danny dove into the aardvark hole, and seconds later, the two horses came past chasing the horse with the cans.

"Come," Danny said, helped the black man on the horse, and they made their way back into the canyon. "Watch out, lots of snakes," Danny said once in with both horses.

"I can't see," the man said.

"Here, I will help you."

Danny ran outside again, grabbed some brush, and covered all the tracks that could show they were inside the hill.

Breaking a branch from the dried thorn tree growing inside with the thorns tearing at his flesh, he shoved it into the narrow entrance.

"Let's hope they won't come back," he said to the black man.

There was no answer. He was lying on the ground exhausted and worn.

As the moons beams ran like small rodents across the vast expanse of the dry countryside, Danny squinted out as far as he could see from his vantage point high on the hill.

Nothing, no sign, whatsoever. He was sure the soldiers thought up some amazing tail to explain their loss and wouldn't think of coming back, least of all to find the black man that outwitted them. It was obvious they would have to figure out a way to get out and get away.

The black man's eyes were swollen, and he could hardly see. That suited Danny fine but didn't want him to see the diamonds.

Rummaging thru the bags and stuff, he got from the soldiers he took stock. Six tins of bully beef, two water bottles, a flint, six candles, binoculars, two knives, two rifles seventy rounds of ammo, one revolver thirty rounds of ammo, a ball of string, and some photos and personal belongings and a map.

"Why you help me?" the black man asked, his eyes swollen shut form the beating.

"Well, I could let you die, or I could use you to help me. Two people have a better chance of making it back to the Boers than one."

"Thanks," the black man replied.

"My name is Daniel," he said.

"My name is Sobuza."

They ate one tin of beef.

"Well, we will have to sit tight looking at this map, we are here, and the main road to Hope town and Kimberly is here. The rail line is here—all of them heavily patrolled." He realized that Sobuza couldn't see a thing he was showing him.

"We need to go east then north. To cross the main road is going to be a problem. To cross the dam river a bigger problem, that is where I got caught last time."

They stayed there for two more days. Danny supplemented their food by catching a few more dassies.

Sobuza could just start to make out movement very faintly when Danny said, "We are going out tonight."

"I looked thru the binoculars, and there is a dried river or gully running parallel to the road in the east, and it swings toward the road. There is a small ridge where we can make our way down into the dried river. It looks about seven to eight feet deep to the bed following the river would place us about thirty yards from the bridge. The patrols pass every thirty minutes if we time it right. We might just get across the road. There is an old ruin of a house about seventy yards north of the bridge, which might give us some shelter who knows."

At dusk they made their way out the bowl. Danny brushed out their tracks but did not place the thorn branch in the gap. "The animals around here must be dying of thirst seeing we have been sitting at their water hole for three days, can't stop them from getting their water. It's theirs in the first place."

The riverbed was sandy dry and looked like a big white ribbon in the moonlight. It quickly became clear that the plan to sneak across was not going to work. The road stretched a good three-fourth of a mile in each direction before it curved.

"Dammit," Danny said, "sure don't want to go back to that hill."

"Didn't you say there was a house about a quarter mile down that way?"

"Yes, but we can't hide there, it's only thirty yards from the road."

"Well, maybe we can set it a light. The soldiers would run there to see what's going on, then we can cross quickly."

Danny knew to light a fire and then get away and not be seen was just about impossible.

"Okay," he said, "I think I can do this. You stay with the horses, keep them quiet. I will be back."

He scurried along the riverbed in the direction where he saw the old house.

Danny stopped, crept up the bank, and peered into the moonlit night. Then he took the binoculars and looked again. There it was about two hundred yards to his right. He had actually gone past it.

Doubling back, he came in line with the house. It was a good fifty yards away. Staying low, he made his way to the back of the house and slipped inside. The roof had collapsed and the dried thatch lay all over. Trying not to make a noise, he started looking around for what he needed. He required one tin fairly large. He found it. What luck, he thought. It had a hole right thru about a third of the way up where someone had shot thru it.

Voices coming closer made him look for a hiding place. He lay on the ground and covered himself best as he could with the thatch.

"Who would want to stay out here?" the voice said.

"Only a dumb Boer."

They laughed.

"Knock, knock, anybody home?" one said as he looked in thru the broken window. Danny saw him clearly thru the thatch.

"O well, nobody here. Let's hit the road again."

The voices faded.

Danny went to work as fast as he could.

He placed the tin on the ground with some of the big rocks that had come out of the wall to hold it upright. Then he tied the string he had with him to one of the rocks, fed it thru the holes in the tin, making sure the entry hole was on the side where the string came out.

Throwing the ball over the roof rafter he then grabbed some thatch, made a bundle, tied it, and ensured that the hanging bundles were right over the tin a good three feet above it.

He pulled the string then let go, the bundle dropped. "Perfect," he said. Placing the candle in the tin, he made sure the string cut into the candle a good inch from the top of the candle. The idea was that once he lit the candle in the tin, it would burn down, burn thru the string, then the bundle would drop into the tin with the candle, and he would have a fire. That's what he hoped would happen. Danny made sure there was a lot of dried wood and thatch around the tin that would make a big fire once the bundle caught fire.

He heard voices again, but they passed by in the road. Once they were gone, he covered the windows to that side of the house as best he could. Lit the candle and made his way back to the dried river, covering his tracks with a dried brush again.

A quick glance back, and if one didn't really look for it would not see the flicker of the candle.

Danny made his way back to Sobuza.

"Hope my plan works," he said out of breath.

They heard the next patrol approached across the little bridge and started off toward the house.

As they were nearing the house one shouted, "What's that fire in the house?"

"Who goes there?" one shouted.

No answer.

Then there was a shot and another.

The soldiers were firing at the house screaming and trying to take cover. Danny and Sobuza wasted no time, was down the last stretch of the river up on the road, and back down into the river in seconds. They never stopped, just kept going.

None of the British soldiers looked back. They were just focused on the burning house and the shots. The never saw the two figures that crossed the road just seventy yards behind them.

"Who was shooting?" Sobuza asked.

"I just placed some of the revolver bullets on the grass. When it caught a light, it got hot and set off the bullets. Well, it seemed to have worked."

The soldiers were still shooting and shouting way in the distance; others had joined them by now.

The riverbed became shallow then flattened out. Danny knew they would have to get cover and quickly it was getting light.

He saw one of the famous Karoo hills to their left. That will have to do. They would see if they could find shelter on the far side away from the road.

There were no canyons, no gullies one fold in the side of the hill that was about ten yards deep "that would have to do," Danny said as the sun's rays raced across the barren land.

Nursing the water from the two bottles they could then wait out the day in the blistering heat.

Danny strung a tarp that was tied to one of the horses out across the fold as best as he could to give shade to them and the two horses.

It helped but barely.

To the north was the river, to the east the Drakensburg Mountains.

"Tonight, we go north, try and get close to the river and water, then we look for cover before the sun is up again."

The river was further than what they thought. Once there, the trees on the banks gave them cover. They drank, washed, and the horses got some well-needed green grass and water. Then they made their way back into the Karoo. Staying at the river was asking for trouble. If the road was patrolled heavily, the river was worse.

A big bunch of trees came into view in the moonlight and they made their way toward them. Thorns scratched stung and pricked them as they made their way into the bunch of trees. Satisfied that they would not be spotted, they waited for the day to break.

"I have a mother and a brother back at my home. I'm Nugni," he said. I haven't seen her maybe since last summer."

"My mother asked me to go find my brother. He had jumped on that steel machine I think they call train, and then he was gone. So I went there, and these bad people, they catch me, beat me, and throw me in that box with the horses. I couldn't understand what they said, but then I see they want me to look after the horses. So I think it's okay once I get to where the train stops. I can go look for my brother Aikona. No, no. They tell me to stay or they shoot me.

"The train went a long way then stop, with lots of men with guns. They didn't feed me, so I sometimes had to eat some of the stuff they left behind when they had eaten. Long time in the winter I was cold, so I slept with the horses to stay warm during the day. I was very, very, very cold.

"Then the train broke just over the river when they were all busy with the train. I ran away, that's when they found me and they beat me Then you saved me.

"Thank you, thank you."

Danny realized that for these people it was even worse. It wasn't their war, yet they were caught up in it and were used by both sides, treated like animals and disposed of like objects.

The trees gave some shade. Danny helped himself to some of the gum from one of the trees.

Sobuza laughed. "You know, you know," he said. "Good."

They had to make sure they weren't sitting on some thorns that would be painful.

Both men spoke about their families, how they loved them, longed to see them, and were frantic and worried about them. Wondering if they were safe?

Danny told Sobuza about the concentration camps—the stories they heard, how people died, and it made him even more worried.

"I was told they did the same to the black people, but they never fed or gave them water, just left them to die," Sobuza said.

"How can people do that?"

"I don't know," Danny shook he's head, "but they will pay for their crimes. God will make them pay."

"What's your mother's name?"

"Nkosi."

"And your daughter?" Sobuza asked

"Hettie. Hettie with the flaming red hair."

"My wife's name is Christina. She's the most beautiful girl in the world."

He spoke about his mom and dad and how he had lost both at a very young age when they drowned while crossing a river. How he was taken in by a store owner in PieterMaritzburg.

When the evening came, they knew they would have to run the gauntlet back to the river, get water, then move east again. Danny's map would take them as far as Norvalspont; after that, they would have to figure it out by themselves.

Crossing the road between Norvalspont and Colesberg was easier. There were much more trees and that gave them cover. Being quite a way from the town helped them not to get the smell of death that lingered in the air from the concentration camp at Norvalspont.

They weren't spared that as they neared Bethulie. At first they weren't sure what it was, only when they topped a hill south of the river at Bethulie and Danny looked with his binoculars did they realize what it was. Danny went berserk. He wanted with all his might to go down there, free the woman and children, single-handed. But it was Sobuza that saved him by knocking him out with a rock.

When he came to with a severe headache, Sobuza said,

"You can't go there even with a whole lot of Boers. They have a lot of the Rooineks there. They would have shot you, and you wouldn't have saved anybody or anything. Don't be stupid."

"My wife and daughter could be in that camp," he shouted at Sobuza.

"I know. But you can't help them, not now."

Danny sat there tears running down his cheeks. "But my wife and daughter could be in there, Sobuza," he said again.

"I know, but we have to live, so we can fight them with more people. We need to be strong to fight them."

It cost Danny all his strength not to swim the river and go look for his love and his daughter.

They moved further east.

As darkness came, they tried to cross the river just below the confluence of the Caledon and Orange rivers.

It was while they came out the river that Sobuza let out a shriek like a girl.

"What the hell," Danny said, "be quiet. You want the Rooineks to hear us?"

"It's a frog a big frog."

"A frog?"

"Come on, it's just a bullfrog, will bite you, and it might hurt or fester, but the bloody thing is harmless. You shrieking like that will have every Rooineck for miles around breathing down our backs."

"My brother. He used to torture me with frogs when I was small. Since then, I am scared of them."

Danny laughed silently.

This man was a Nugi warrior and was afraid of frogs.

As they sat there drying, Danny noticed a mark on the back of Sobuza's leg, shaped like a big z.

"What's that?" he asked.

"My brother. He had stabbed me with a spear, nearly lost my leg."

"This brother of yours, he doesn't like you, does he?"

"No," Sobuza answered.

Constantly on the lookout, they skirted towns and roads wherever they could. They would dart into a town undercover of night, stole whatever food they could find, then hightailed it back to cover.

Ficksburg, a town on the border of Basutoland and the Orange Free State, was not too far from Danny's farm, Klien Bakawaan Stad.

He kept his eyes and ears open, looking, watching, and seeing if he could see any boers that could possibly lead him to De Wit.

The Darkensburg foothills around Ficksburg are magnificent with buttresses, sheer cliffs, and undulating grass fields and the occasional clump of trees.

"I have to go east, Danny," Sobuza said. "My village is that way I can't go north."

"You will not make it on your own, Sobuza, stay with me till we meet up with De Wit if we can, then we will see what they say and how you can get back to your village. Wherever that may be. You did say you weren't Zulu."

"No, I'm Swazi Nugni," Sobuza said.

"O now, you tell me, I know where that is, that's on the northern part of Natal. Yes, you would have to move northeast to reach your home."

"I have to go, Danny," Sobuza said. "I have to."

"We are better off if we are two people," Danny tried convincing him.

"Yes, but I must go."

"Okay, here, take one gun some ammo, water, food, and a horse but be very careful. The road between the Transvaal and Natal is even worse than the road between the Cape and Kimberly."

Giving a rifle to a black man was something Danny's Boer friends would certainly not have taken too at all. Never arm a black they would have said. Never.

With that, Sobuza left late that afternoon.

"Who knows we might meet up one day?" Danny said.

"Thanks again for saving my life. I will always be in your debt if you ever come to Swazi land you find me."

The two horsemen were riding like the devil was chasing them. Danny watched from his perch way up on one of the hills thru the binoculars.

About three hundred yards behind them were about fifteen Rooineks giving chase.

They disappeared behind an outcrop and then never reappeared on the other side. The Rooineks flew around the outcrop, and Danny saw them come out the other side a few minutes later and kept going.

Struggling up the hillside, he eventually saw them. They were actually going to crest about one hundred yards from where he was.

"If I was a Rooineck, I could just shoot you both," he said loudly. The two men jumped and grabbed their rifles.

"Hey, I am a Boer like you," he said in Dutch again.

"Bloody hell, man, we thought we were done for," one of the men said.

They came up on to the hill thru the narrow crevasse they had just lumber up in.

"Can you believe it, Danny Venter?" said Frans Decker.

"Danny Venter. How are you, man?" the two men hugged and laughed.

"What in god's name are you doing here?"

Danny related he's adventure to them.

"Were you guys going to?"

"Back to De Wit, we were scouting."

"I going with," Danny said.

"Come let's get out of here before those Rooinecks pick up our tracks."

As they rode, Danny asked about Frans's family and if he knew anything about Christina and Hettie."

"Last I heard, Danny, your farm was burnt down, and Christina and Hettie were taken to the camp in Bloemfontein."

Danny cringed as he thought of the images he had seen thru the binoculars of the camp at Bethulie.

"Donner Bliksem," he swore.

They came to the camp

Who is there?" the voice said.

"It's Frans Gert and Danny."

Once inside the perimeter of De Wit's camp, Danny was summoned to the general.

He told what he has seen on his trip thru the Karoo. The English movements and patrols.

How many men he thought were at Zastron Rouxville Ladybrandt and Wepener.

The mountains and hills around Ficksburg and the outskirts of Bethlehem gave De Wit the cover and escape routes he required, to carry out he's guerrilla warfare.

"When do we take them on?" Danny wanted to know.

"Not so fast, young man. The way we do it is go in, hit hard, take what we can, and disappear."

"There are no more big battles like Maggerfontain or Spioenkop."

Danny was disappointed. He wanted to go in and kill every Rooineck he could find, chase them form this country, find Christina and Hettie, and live in peace.

They camped out on top of ridges all over the countryside. But never in the same place twice.

As early morning broke, a young boy ran into De Wit's tent.

"We are surrounded, General. The British had found us. They are all around us, we are doomed."

"Slowly, young man, slowly. Let's go see what's going on." Skirting the perimeter, it became obvious they were surrounded on all sides.

The enemy had shelter, plenty of trees, and rocks were abundant cover.

"How did this happen? Who was on guard, why did we not see them coming?"

"They came last night under cover of darkness, General. We would never have known. We couldn't see them coming. It was a dark moon last night."

It didn't take long for the British to start shelling the camp Shrapnel wized about like bees.

The Boers fired back with no real effect. The Rooineks had a big advantage, but firing back made the shelling less intense.

The general called his men together. "I want those guns silenced. Aim and shoot as good as you can. Pieter, how much ammunition do we have?"

"We have about three thousand rounds, General."

"Bliksem."

The cannon had been placed in a clearing between some trees. About five hundred yards away standing in some long grass, the field canon was firing rounds at will. Taking careful aim, Danny judged the distance elevation and wind then after he set the sites on his .303 he fired. The British soldier tumbled backward sending the rest of his mates scurrying for cover, leaving the Canon in the open.

"Good shot," Frans said to Danny.

Did not take long for Danny to be called; they needed him at other locations to stop those attending the canons. Danny taught himself how to handle a gun when he worked for Mr. McKintosh in his store in PieterMaritzburg. Would take the rifles out back to show buyers how they worked and what they could do. Let them shoot some targets. He loved the Enfield.303.

At night it was a different story. The British soldiers could man the guns and shelled away at leisure.

"We have to get of this hill, or they will kill us all," De Wit said.

"But how, General?"

He sat for a while, thinking.

This man was a ghost. The British could never catch him. He was way too elusive and too cunning.

"Where is the most open area around this hill?"

"That would be here," the man said. They had drawn a map in the sand showing the canons and British locations.

"Okay that's where we will descend."

"What?"

"The British would never expect us to go that way. They will be waiting in the trees and rocks for us, but here they would think it foolish and foolish we will be."

"General, we will be killed. There is no cover, sir."

"Exactly! Who in his right mind would go that way?"

"Tonight make sure all the horses' feet are padded with grass, tie branches to them to stop them being recognized. Then we have to silence those canons somehow. Don't want them flashing all night will make us visible to the eye. Don't want that."

"We have that new man, Daniel. He seems to be quite a marksman, sir."

"Call him."

Danny stood in front of De Wit. His small tent is white ragged and very sparsely furnished, one table a fold-up chair and a field bed.

"I hear you are quite marksman. Would you be able to keep the British away from the canons for an hour or so?"

"Yes, sir."

"No man tonight."

"I wouldn't be able to see them," Danny said," that would be very difficult, sir."

"We can look at where the guns are flashing and shoot in that direction, but they would already be at the canons, sir."

"I know. Is there any way we can shoot at them in the dark and stop them manning the canons?"

"I don't know." Danny was thinking hard.

"Well, maybe, sir. Let me try. I will be back."

Danny asked Frans to help him, ducking thru the rocks with the shrapnel flying all around, they made their way to the trees on the summit. They came to the spot where he shot that first soldier.

The shells from the canons were relentless.

Smoke and shrapnel flew all over.

"I need a stick, a long stick. Just get me a stick."

"Here. Will this do?"

"Yes, get your knife."

"Why?"

"Just get your damn knife," Danny said irritated.

"Okay, okay."

"First let me get them away from the canon."

"Now, I am going to aim at that rock where they are hiding, just to the left side, so if someone thought of making their way back to the canon, it would be like I was shooting at them okay."

"When I'm perfectly on the spot,I will fire. If I hit it, I will stand as still as possible. Then I want you to shove that stick in the ground and cut it perfectly to fit under the rifle butt right here."

"Yes."

Danny took aim. The shot wined as it hit the rock.

Frans shoved the stick in the ground under Danny's rifle, then cutting it perfectly placed it in under the butt. Then he said to Frans, "Now take some charcoal and mark the spot here on the rock were the rifle was resting."

"Make sure that stick can't move. It can't move anywhere," Danny said.

He placed some big rocks around the base of the stick.

"Bring your rifle now, place the butt on the stick right here like that. The front end here where I made the mark with the charcoal."

"Fire."

The shot was followed by the wine of the bullet hitting the rocks where the British soldiers were taking cover.

"If we do that with all the locations, four men could fire at night at the locations where the British are hiding, stopping them from manning the canons."

"A Boer makes a plan," Frans smiled.

"What I will do is place something better here where we made the mark on the rock so we don't have to try and figure out exactly were in the dark."

"Good work," De Wit said. "Want everybody loaded up and ready to leave just after dark if we're lucky. There will be a lot of cloud, and the moon will rise quite late.

Five men will man the positions firing at those British hideouts next to the canons every two minutes. While they're firing, we will thread the needle and make our way down the mountain.

And God help us. Those five men will have to make it down by foot.

You know of course that the British will know something's wrong if we stop shooting any suggestions.

"Well, sir," Jasper, one of the men, said, "I think I can help."

A shell exploded a few yards outside the tent.

"Shit, that was close.'

"I need about twenty cans. We fill them all with different amounts of water, place them around the fire, and place a revolver bullet in each when the water boils off. The can will get hot, the bullet will go off, but no one will be there and the British will be none the wiser."

De Witt laughed. "That's why we are Boers, we always make a plan."

When the sun went down and Danny saw the first movement by the Rooinecks to man the canons, he started firing, so did the others. He and the other four placed their guns on those sticks and started to fire. There was no canon fire; it worked.

"How the hell do they see in the dark?"

"How am I supposed to know, but I am not going near that cannon?" Just then, the next shot wined off the rock inches from the soldier's head.

"Bloody hell." The cowered behind the rock.

As the five men crawled down the hill, the first shot in the can went off. Frans bumped Danny's arm, showed him thumbs up in the dark.

It was feats like this that made the British ever so frightened of De Wit. He was surrounded and still got away how the hell did he do it.

Unfortunately it was all in vain as they all were summoned to Vereeniging by the Boer Republic to lay down arms and surrender only two months later.

De Witt broke his rifle refusing to give a good weapon to the British. Danny took out the bridge lock from the Martini Henry and then the bolt from the .303 and threw the rifles on the pile with the rest. The rifles would be useless without its firing mechanism.

There was just one thing on his mind. He had to get to Bloemfontein and quick.

It would take him four days of hard riding before he would get there. He had no idea if he was going to find Christina and Hettie alive.

CHAPTER 2

The day Danny left Christina was beside herself. She knew that there was no alternative if the Boer republics were to survive. Every available man would have to go and fight in the war.

As he reached the hill, Danny looked back at his farm. He saw the small patch of corn to the left, a willow tree about 230 yards off to the right, and the small dirt road leading to their house.

Thatch roof brown walls made of mud and clay. The two figures, Christina and Hettie, just on three years old standing in front of the house. Even at this distance, her flaming red hair could be seen.

His heart screamed "go back," but his loyalty to his country said "go" and he was gone.

Word quickly spread around. The British were clearing out the farms, taking the woman and children to camps. They went about burning crops and houses, taking everything, leaving nothing. Part of Lord Roberts scorched earth policy. Get the woman of the farms so the Boers can't get food or help.

Word had reach Christina by some of the black people that the British go from farm to farm grab the people and burn down the building then put poison in the water.

She knew they were coming, just didn't know when. She grabbed the shovel and dug a deep pit about twenty yards behind the house filled one of the trunks, they had with provisions and a revolver, an ax and a small bag of corn, which she placed in a big tin then placed a lid on it. Covering it with some planks she placed some dirt and tufts of grass on it. As fast as she could, she ran back to the front of the house and dug a hole in the soft earth about three feet deep and three feet round. Lining it with some old cloth and clay, she then filled some canisters with water and filled it up.

Going to the actual well, she covered that with branches and grass and obscured the track to the well. She was just pouring in the last bucket of water when they came. There were eight of them—six whites and two blacks.

They came in, dragged her and Hettie to one side—screaming, shouting, and then set the house on fire, poured poison into her fake well, shot the dog, and after looking the donkey over shot it as well. A tragedy one could say, but this was just the beginning of one man's evil.

Breton Winslow was a man that would make a demon flinch. There are no words known to man that would do justice to describe this thing some would call a man.

Blond, he was not very muscular and of average height. Golden eyes like some snake. A big evil smile that looked normal. At first glance, he seemed quite respectable, but it would take less than a second to change that.

A spoiled boy raised on the moors of the Midlands and living the life of the rich. He stood there as though he was watching a masterpiece painted by some world-renowned painter.

But he had more evil to give. He loved to let his men rape the Boer women, seven of them, and then he would decide if she lived or died.

"Let me have her, Sergeant, I haven't had a woman in days. That last woman you said I could have just jumped in to the flames, remember?"

"O, I do. Wasn't that something beautiful to behold? She screaming, the flames engulfing her like a lover, then the whooshing as she wet herself in the flames. Was just so beautiful."

"Please, Sergeant, let me have her," Donald Black said.

Christina never let on that she could understand English. But what she heard was as good as being told she was going to be shot.

"Let's have some fun, boys," he shouted to the men.

The men gathered around Christina. She had nowhere to go.

She was terrified for herself and Hettie.

Hettie was crying and screaming.

Breton walked over, and without blinking an eye lifted her by her long red hair dangling her in the air. She screamed with pain. He then threw her into the back of the wagon they had brought with them. He smiled at her and placed his finger on his lips. The small girl, barely four years old, lay there scared to the point of death.

"No more screaming, okay?"

The child was close to fainting from sheer terror and fright.

Christina tried to help her but was thrown back by the circle of men.

She had grown up on a farm in the clay pits area of the eastern border of the Cape Province. The Mahoney farm it was called.

Her grandfather quickly realized he wouldn't make it as a farmer and started transporting of goods. Her grandmother was Irish born, outside the town of Langford. Survived the British and eventually immigrated to Africa when the big famine came to Ireland.

A single girl amongst four boys, she never had it easy had to fight for what was hers and had to defend herself regardless of the fact the she was the middle child and a girl.

Donald Black who had asked Breton if he could have her came forward then he slapped her. She never flinched, just watched him. He was surprised by this.

"O boy, this one is tough," he said, "she's going to be a good one."

As he looked at the men around him, Christina took her chance hit him with her fist. She caught him below the left eye, and he stumbled then fell to the ground holding his cheek dizzy.

"What a useless shit you are. Let me get her," another man said and walked toward her.

He hit her with his fist. She stumbled but held her ground.

"Look at that this. This lady is really a tough one. She's going to be good to have."

Then he rushed her and grabbed both her hands.

She leaned forward his face right in her face and bit his nose. He let go and fell back.

The small circle of men was having a good time. This was more fun than they expected. The ground was bare and dusty.

"Shit," one of the other men said, "we have a real tiger here."

He grabbed her from behind when she backed off from the man she bit. She never saw it coming.

"Now we have you, let's see what you can do." He was making sexual movements with his pelvis.

Christina bent forward then snapped her head back catching him full in the face blood exploded from he's broken nose and even splatter on some of the other men.

If they were going to rape her, she wasn't going to just let them take her. This cannot be happening. She thought, *This is not happening.*

Amongst the men was a big soldier about six-two. Strong in build, a big black beard.

Let a man show you how it's done.

He came toward her. She hit him in the face with her fist, then again, he just laughed.

"You will have to do better than that, my love," he said.

His big muscled arms clamped around her waist as he lifted her off the ground squeezing the air from her and causing her a lot of pain.

"What lovely breasts," he said and buried he's head in her bosom

Cupping her hands, she opened them wide then slapped the cups of her hands on both ears. He screamed and backed off kneeling on the ground holding his head.

"Enough of this. We don't have all day," Breton said.

"Now, my lady, you'll get undressed. My men will have their way with you or I will slit this lovely child's throat." He placed the knife against Hettie's throat, and it drew blood.

Christina screamed, "You bunch of animals." She said in Dutch, "You pigs."

He laughed.

He walked over, took his knife, and one by one cut the ribbons of the front of her dress. Then forcibly pushed her on to the ground opening her dress to reveal her breasts. "Now look at that," he said.

"Sergeant, a rider is coming."

"Who is it?"

"Don't know, but he's got a black uniform."

"Fuck it's an officer."

"Come let's getting moving here."

As she collapsed on the ground, Christina covered herself and was crying uncontrollably.

The man in the black uniform climbed off his horse.

"Sergeant," he answered Breton saluted.

"Sergeant Winslow," he said.

"I heard a woman screaming, Sergeant, what was that about?"

"This woman is total mad, sir, we had to try and control her. Look what she did to my men."

He walked over to Christina.

"Let me help you up, madam," he said.

"O dear, look at your dress. If I may, let me dust of the back here."

"You there find this lady a coat to cover herself," he said.

As the sun warmed the earth on a lovely morning bringing with it the wonder of God's creation, this man and his kindness brought that to Christina.

She stumbled to the wagon. The major helped her on to it where she took Hettie in her arms.

Hettie was in complete shock. "Sergeant, bring me some water."

Winslow very begrudgingly handed the major a canteen.

"Here, my dear, have some water, let me look at the blood on your head," he said. He washed of some of the blood. Then he looked at her head; some of the hair had torn from the scalp where Winslow had lifted her up.

Walking as though he was on a Sunday stroll next to a beautiful lake, he came up to Winslow.

Like lighting, he grabbed Winslow by the front of his tunic and lifted him up.

"Sergeant, my name is Patrick Murray. Now the name Murray is Irish for Lord or master. My rank was a gift from a noble gentleman by names Mister Fitzroy Macy for catching the man that killed his son.

"I cut my teeth as a constable in the shit and mud and crap in the docks of Liverpool. Became a chief constable they feared me down at the docks I was and will always be the lord of justice they said."

"Let's see the lady is mad yet she lay on her back and the front of her dress had been cut with a knife. How did she do that, Sergeant?"

Winslow was going to answer when the major placed his finger on Winslow's lips still holding him up with his other hand.

"Now the little girl, lovely little thing, bright red hair, blue eyes. There must be some Irish in there somewhere for sure."

"She fell into the wagon. I presume then her hair got stuck somehow, and she tried to pull herself free that's why her hair has been pulled out.

"Or maybe, just maybe, someone lifted her by her hair and threw her into the wagon that's why she has a nasty bruise on her elbow and a mark on her throat."

He let go of Winslow and turned to the men who stood there wide-eyed.

"You bunch of worthless snake shit slime. I know the likes of you. I have seen the likes of you, and let's not forget, I saw eleven of the likes of you hung," Then he smiled. "And who knows before the month is out, I would make that an even dozen by having one of you wonderful soldiers court-martial-ed and shot. I would do that myself with my trusted webbly."

"There have been rumors that some Boer women have been raped beaten and savaged by British soldiers. Correct me if I might be wrong, Sergeant." he turned back to Winslow.

Just like the sun could warm you and show you God's creation, the look in Patrick Murray's eyes was a blistering hot sun in a desert burning flesh from skin.

"We represent Queen Victoria, fighting under her royal banner, and we conduct ourselves as her troops, royal troops if I might say so."

He raised his gun and placed it on the tip of Winslow's nose. "You tell me, Sergeant, again please. This lady went mad then cut her own dress, lifted her own kid by the hair, and flung her into that wagon. Am I right?"

Winslow never answered. Evil knows little or shows little fear, only hate.

"O I have seen that look before, Sergeant. Believe me I have. Doesn't do anything for me though, just makes me more determined to rid this place of people like you."

"I want these injured men and you in my tent in Bloemfontein when we get there."

Bloemfontein was the capital of the old Boer republic of the Orange Free State. It was taken over by the British and was one of their main staging posts and headquarters.

"The lady, her child, and all the other prisoners will be in good health when we get there. Am I understood, Sergeant?" he said as he pulled back the hammer on the Webbly.

Winslow closed his eyes.

"Fully, sir" he hissed, then saluted.

The major cradled his revolver then saluted him back.

Turning to Christina and Hettie, he lifted his helmet and said, "Good day to you too, ladies."

He climbed on his horse. Then bellowed, "Let's get going."

Winslow made sure that Christina and Hettie knew that they will be in a camp and that no one would know if they disappeared. So if she said anything, one of his men would make sure that first Hettie then she would come to a gruesome and untimely end. It took them more than a week to reach Bloemfontein.

The smell of the camp came to them long before they reached it. It was March 1900. The camp had been there for close on eighteen months. Sprawled on a hillside, the camp was in two sections: the old camp and the new camp. Christina and Hettie were in the new camp. This was a blessing as the old camp was the worst of the two. It helped. Situated on the outskirts of Bloemfontein on a barren hillside with no water at all, it was a place to die.

There were rows and rows of tents, some had cots, but most people slept on the bare ground.

Christina gasped when she saw the inmates walking around looking like skeletons. A wagon load of naked corpses came by with some followers. No one cried. Mostly children they were being taken to the far side of the camp where there was row on row of small crosses. The stench of despair and death hung in the air like banners at a parade clinging to the skin like sticky sweat at the sea. It made hell look like a ballroom set for a wedding.

She said nothing at the inquiry, although Major Murray tried to convince her she would not be brought to harm. Winslow and his men walked free.

This death camp was the place where someone like Winslow could live thrive and blossom. He could indulge in his evil like a hungry man at a feast.

Lucifer and his angels, the people called him.

Breton Winslow, Donald Black, and Patrick Peal—they thrived in the misery and pain of those around them. To complain amplified the pain and suffering to that individual ten times over.

Christina quickly realized that the camp population was mostly women and children, old men and old woman.

She had been attacked when she entered by a swarm of people asking if she had any food. She gave then some but had made sure she hid the majority away.

The tent she was allocated was swarming with flies. Vomit and feces were on the ground and side of the tent. Blood and some ungodly liquid covered the one-camp cot.

She staggered back. "This can't be real," she gasped.

"Maria van Staden," the old woman said as she walked up.

"The old woman was the last to go. We only realized she had died three days after she was dead."

Christina Venter replied. "This cannot be where we must live."

"It is, my dear. Mine was worse when I came. There were parts of the boy's flesh stuck to the cot when I got it."

She thought she was going to be sick.

"Don't worry you'll get used to it," the old woman said.

"You're in luck. Looks like rain in about an hour. Just drag the cots out and wash them off with mud, then leave them out for a day or two in the sun. They will be okay."

As she sat there on the trunk, Hettie beside her, she feared they were going to die here. She and her kid and Danny wouldn't even know. There would be no name on a grave, just a number out there on that piece of ground. What made her even more fearful was what would happen if she died first and Hettie was alone in this place. She prayed that God would help them and keep them safe and alive.

The rain turned to hail. She went out in the cold and hail. Using the mud and ice from the hail, she scrubbed both cots both sides and the legs as best she could. Placed them where she could see them to be drenched and further washed by the rain. Taking a big pot from her trunk, she placed it outside to fill with water.

"Now, lassie, let me tell you something," her grandma had said.

"Stay clean. Never shit were the sick shit." She remembers her mother saying that the grandmother should not talk like that in front of the kids.

"And look, there is food everywhere if you look. Make plans, and most of all make provision, for tomorrow there might really be nothing."

It took a week of cleaning and scrubbing the tent, sweeping the floors before Christina was satisfied that the tent was somewhat livable.

The Orange Free State has dramatic seasons. Summers that were from hell and winters from the arctic.

When she sat there in her tent in the sweltering heat eating the little half ration she had gotten, her dad's voice came to her. *That bloody Karoo, my child, it can get warm, so warm that you couldn't leave a metal object outside as it would burn you blisters if you tried to pick it up after an half hour in the sun.*

"As for the winters," he said.

"Snow sometimes and very, very cold." Her dad had made them help unpack the wagon after a trip and erect the tent. He had to make sure it was still okay and do repairs.

"The entrance away from the prevailing winds."

They had to wash the mud of the sides of the tent. "What's all the mud on the inside of the tent, Dad?" she asked.

"Now, little girl, when it gets cold, the wind blows and then blows thru the fabric of the tent. But if you had some good clay mud like you would find in an ant heap, you could smear the inside of the tent on the bottom when there is still some sun. Then it can harden. That way you could keep some of that cold wind out of the tent."

"Always dig a deep trench around the tent so the rainwater wouldn't run into the tent but around it keeping the tent dry."

She knew that head lice would be a problem as they couldn't wash or bathe. Using the sharp knife she had hidden, she shaved off both her and Hettie's hair completely. Hettie protested like mad. They looked ghastly, but she knew they had to do it.

Others saw what she was doing and came to ask. She told them not thinking much of it. Within a few weeks, people close to her tent would come for advice.

It would have been hard, it would have been living in a grave waiting for death, and it all would have been unbearable. Yet it was Breton Winslow. Every day, every moment in his presence was being undressed by the devil himself. Although some were allowed passes to get into town to buy food, this was not the case with Winslow and his section.

Anna Combrink's son was dreadfully ill, probably typhoid fever. She begged for medicine.

"Please, Sergeant, my boy is ill, just want something I can't help him. He's very ill," she said.

Don't have any he said and walked off.

The next morning he brought with him a small blue bottle.

"Who was the lady that asked for something for her son?"

Anna Combrink surged thru the people and shouted, "It was me."

"Here," he said. "Take this. It will help."

She took the small bottle of medicine and made her way to her son in the tent shivering with fever on his cot.

She gave him the medicine. Within seconds, he convulsed wrenching, screaming with pain to die within a minute.

Screaming she came back to Breton.

"The medicine you gave me was poison."

"No, no. It wasn't medicine, never said it was. I only said it would help, that's what I said. It did. He's dead, no more suffering." He laughed, not an evil laugh, just the same laugh someone would laugh hearing a good joke.

"You killed him," she shouted.

"Sorry, I never gave him the stuff. You did. You killed your own son, my dear. You gave him the poison."

This time he laughed so much he had tears in his eyes.

Anna Combrink died the next day, the guilt the pain of killing her own son just drained the life form her like a leaking water bag.

"What a pity," Breton said the next day

"Well, at least, she's with her son now." He smiled. "That's good news," he said.

His two angels nodded their heads trying to act sincere.

Food was scarce, very scares. Ration tickets were issued. The rations they did get was either frozen solid or lased with blue vitriol, a substance that would make one sick induce diarrhea. For someone weak and lacking nutrition, this was a death sentence.

"Have to look for food," Christina remembered what the grandmother had said.

"Termites make a tasty meal," her dad had said. If you open the nest to get the mud for your tent, the white ones are good. Just watch out for the redhead devils, they bite, and it burns like hell."

Getting the mud and the termites lasted about two days. Word got out, and the anthill she had found was now a hole in the ground. She collected the dried ground that was once the hill shaking her head.

She longed for Danny, feared that he might be dead, and she would never know. Dreams and hope keeps one alive. It is a food that can sustain when nothing else can. She dreamed that this would end, and they will be back at the farm.

A bitter cold winter's morning, and Breton had everybody lined up for food ration tickets.

They were standing there with cups of hot tea, drinking the steaming hot liquid while people came past.

Anna Brandt, a young girl about nine, was standing there looking at them when Winslow asked her if she wanted some tea.

"You want some tea, my girl?"

"Yes," she said.

A small girl skinny frail with big brown eyes.

"Come, come."

She walked over.

"Once she was in reach, he grabbed her arm violently."

Then while holding her poured the steaming hot tea over her frail little hand.

She screamed in pain and struggle to free herself, but he made sure he held her tight until he emptied the cup slowly over her hand.

Blisters appeared within an instant

She ran back to her mother holding her hand screaming with pain.

No one said a word.

Breton laughed his typical everyday laugh.

"She did ask for tea, so I gave her some."

Christina wowed that God should spare her and Hettie so she could kill this man one day.

As the days passed into months and more people died of disease and of ill health, lack of food, Christina was sure they would die here in this sewage hole of life.

Hettie sat on the bed. "Mom when you think we will die?"

"I don't know, Hettie, when we are old maybe."

"No, Mom, when like this week or next week. I see everybody dies, so we will die soon too, I know."

"No, no, Hettie, we will not. I will make sure we will live whatever it takes."

"Please, Mom, let me die first. I don't want to be in this place alone, promise."

Fear, fear, and despair filled her being. But it was the hate, the hate for Winslow and his men that kept her going.

Her heart was full, but she never cried. She just held on to Hettie as though she were never going to go away her skeleton like body hard against the bones of her own.

People never seem to learn or realize that you can't trust the devil.

An eight years old, Fanus Britz, wanted to be in the field with his dad and grandpa, but he was carted off to the camp. He hated it. He was a man in his eyes and not a little boy.

"Today is Christmas, so I have a present here for someone. A lovely loaf of bread," the devil spoke.

But to get this present, you would have to give me something.

"Fuck off," Fanus shouted. His mom hit him hard against the head.

"Watch your mouth," she said.

Breton came down the line to the boy.

He grabbed him and dragged him to his table were the ration tickets were issued.

"You are a brave one," he said.

The little boy tried to be a man. His brown dusty hair and gray features and green eyes glared at Winslow with hate.

"I hate you, Rooinecks."

"O that's good. I hate the Boers. That makes us the same."

"Now let's see if you're that brave. What would you do to get this bread?"

Fanus said nothing.

"I know."

He grabbed hold of Fanus, dragging him kicking and screaming to the table where they had been sitting. He took the boy's hand and placed it on the table and then took out his knife.

"Let's see if you're brave enough to give me a finger for the bread."

"Fuck you," again Fanus swore.

His mom was pleading to Breton to let the boy go.

"He's only a child. Let him go, please."

She was held back by Patrick and Donald.

It took him more than five minutes to cut off the little boy's pinkie.

Donald and Patrick kept the crowd at bay with their guns loaded and ready to fire.

Fanus's mother was going mad. Others held her back to stop her from being shot.

The pain made the boy pee his pants and then he passed out.

Once done Breton let him fall to the ground then threw the finger to a mangy dog that was standing there that ate it in one bite.

As though he was doing something very good and special, he went to the mother then breaking the moldy old bread in half gave it to her and said, "Merry Christmas to you too, ma'am. It was only a pinkie, so only half a bread."

He threw the rest of the bread to the dog. All three laughed aloud.

"Come, come, let's get you your food rations," they said as though nothing happened.

Every deed he did, every evil plan, every horror he devised was like a cancer eating at Christina's soul. She wanted him to suffer and die. To make him pay for what he was doing to this defenseless people. But she could do nothing, just watch.

Rumors started to circulate thru the camp that the war was ending, that the Boers were surrendering.

If this brought hope to the inmates, it brought urgency to Breton to do more and more evil.

"It has come to my attention that your husbands are surrendering and will be her soon to come get you. So I decided that we will not waste our rations. We will wait for them to bring you some food."

"Only one ration a week."

The graveyard was a long distance from the camp. The wagon load of corpses, some babies in soap boxes that double as coffins, were taken there every day.

Taking the old cloth, the woman was wrapped in from the body. Breton with his white cloves lifted her hand then in a waving motion waved it to the mourners that followed.

"Good-bye," he said smiling.

"I have decided that we need to make some changes, so no one will be able to go to the old camp, and for the next week, we need to get you excited, your spirits up, so when your husbands arrive, if they are alive or not, who knows they might be on some camp in St. Helena or Ceylon somewhere. Those that aren't will be here soon, so we need to cheer them up so we will practice to sing 'God Save the Queen' every day."

It sounded harmless, but he made them stand outside in the elements for hours singing every day draining there bodies of every little bit of nourishment it still had left.

Christina and Hettie were dying. They knew that unless they got some food, they would not survive another week.

The noise that came from town could be heard all the way at the camp.

"What's going on?" one asked.

"It's over. Everybody surrendered in Vereeniging (town in the Transvaal), even De Wit the war is over."

Breton and his friends made sure that everybody knew that Britain had won.

When the first Boers started arriving two days later and the stories of their evil deeds were told, they vanished. No one knew where or how; they were just gone.

Although some of the people in town tried to help those in the camps with some food, many just stayed away for fear of contracting disease.

Christina begged and scrounged everywhere for any morsel of food and water. They had some water but very little or no food.

As she sat there, outside the tent, she cried that now that it was over, she and Hettie would die never knowing if her love her Danny was alive or not.

The voice that came from afar sounded familiar. "Christina, Christina!"

Someone was calling her name.

She stood up to see who it was. A man with a horse, big beard, scrawny, was coming down the rows of tents, screaming her name. *Who was this?* Someone with news about Danny.

She waved. "Here," she said uncertain.

"Here I'm Christina.

When he saw her, he ran. "You're alive, thank God, you're alive."

"Danny? Danny? Danny?" Then she cried.

"Where is Hettie? Please tell me Hettie is alive."

"In the tent."

He rushed in. The little skeleton on the bed looked at him but did not recognize him.

"Hettie," he said hugging her, feeling the frail bones in his arms.

"Danny, we haven't had any food for more than a week," Christina said.

Danny rushed to his horse, opened the saddlebag, then returned with four tins of bully beef, two pieces of biltong, and a few rusks. (biltong is jerky)

"Here, here," he said, "Eat. Just take it slow."

Hettie slowly sucked on the hard rusk to get it soft enough to eat.

Danny poured some water in a can then soaked the rest of the rusks to make a porridge.

She ate it quickly.

Christina ate some bully beef, and Danny sliced them some biltong.

"Thank God," he said. "You're alive. Thank god."

"Barely," Christina looked at him. "What a mess we are. Look at us," she said.

"Who the hell cares? We're alive, and we are together."

Klein Bakawaan Stad near Singers Post that's where they wanted to be as far as they could be from this evil place.

Instead of traveling north, Danny just cut straight across the veldt to Lindely and Singers Post.

About four miles out of town, they came across a small stream. Danny stopped and then he said to Christina and Hettie, "Here, take this shirt, use it as a towel, I have a small piece of blue soap. You and Hettie, have a lovely bath."

Although the water was cold, the two of them washed the dirt of as though they were washing off the memories of that filthy place. Danny didn't watch. No, he walked upstream fed the horse, had it drink, filled both water bottles. And started looking for whatever they could eat.

He found two big crabs and caught a reasonable catfish that he speared with a reed.

They made a fire so that the two woman could dry their clothes or what was left of their clothes, and he cooked the meager meal.

"Thanks," she said.

"Hey, we have to eat."

"No," she said, "not the food."

"What?"

"For not looking at me when I bathed. I look awful, and the shame would have been unbearable."

"You are beautiful, Christina. You are and will always be beautiful."

"Liar," she said, but she felt good for him saying it.

"Thanks though." She smiled.

Her first smile in more than a year.

It would be a ten-day journey. The countryside was strewn with burnt farms that had been looted.

Passing a house they saw someone sitting against the wall.

Danny walked over.

"Good day," he said.

The old woman stood up. "Good day," she said, Gertruida vander Merwe."

"Danny Venter, my wife Christina, my daughter Hettie."

"Please to meet you," she said.

"What are you doing out here, are you alone?"

"Yes, I am. Came from Norvalspont with the Allermans. They dropped me here. I hoped my sons would be here, but they weren't."

"You can't stay here by yourself. It's not safe," Christina said.

"What can I do?"

"You're coming with us. That's that."

"But what if my sons come?"

"We will leave a note," Danny said.

He scribbled a notice on the side of the building with a burnout piece of wood. It stated that Gertruida had gone with them and they should look for her further down the line at the farms along the road.

"Is that okay?" Danny asked.

"I think so."

"Come, let's go. Is there anything here you want to take with you?"

She looked at the ruin. "No." She said, "Nothing. Just this bag."

That was what happened all over. People, returned to nothing—no families, no husbands, no children, and no farms. All had been destroyed. In one foul movement, a whole generation had been obliterated.

The man working on the house saw them coming and walked over. They went thru the formalities of introductions.

"Yes, I rode with De Laroi."

"De Wit."

"Bloody mess, man."

"We have a small problem. See, this old lady, she's from two farms down. She hoped her sons would be on the farm, but there was nobody there. We didn't want to just leave her there, so we brought her with us. What I need to ask is if she can stay here until her family can come and get her when they get back? I scribbled a note on the building asking them to check on the farms down the road?"

"I really don't know, man."

"I can cook. I can sow. I can wash," Gertruida piped up.

"Well, that can help. I am a useless cook."

"Just no hanky-panky."

They all burst out laughing.

When they left, they felt good. They knew she was in good hands, and they also knew that the man needed someone to talk to for companionship.

As they came over the rise of the hill where the road wound down to their house, they stopped. The house was burned down, but the walls were still standing.

The lonely willow tree was off to their right, and the veldt had struggled to come back after it had been burned down. No one said a word as they made their way down to the house from the top of the hill a good four hundred yards away.

It was Hettie that spoke first.

"What a big mess, hey, Mom? We will just have to clean up, make it nice and pretty again."

"We will," Christina said.

Danny walked thru what was once the front door to find that the one wall inside the house had collapsed. Using his fist, he knocked the walls.

They were black from the fire, burned wood lay all over. Grass had started to grow on what was once the floor. "Actually, Christina, as stupid as this may sound, the fire did good. It baked the walls rock hard."

"O well I will have to see what we can do about some food. Just wish I had something to go shoot some game with." Danny said.

She walked away from the house to the patch she knew was there.

"Where you going, Christina?"

She didn't answer.

Then brushing away the dirt, she found the wooden planks. She smiled.

"What you up to?" Danny asked again.

"Come help, and you will see."

Danny and Hettie helped get the dirt out the way and then lifted the planks.

"What's this?" Danny said.

"Help me," Christina said as she lifted out one trunk and then the other.

It was all there just like she had packed it. She laughed. Tears flowed down her cheeks.

"I fooled the bastard," she said. "I fooled him."

"Look at this Sergeant Winslow."

Danny was amazed at what she had stored: the food, the revolver, everything.

"Christina, you're amazing," he said.

She smiled back. Her hair had started to grow back, and she had a boyish look about her.

It took them a few weeks to rebuild the farm and get it liveable again; thankfully it only rained after they had the roof thatched.

Food was still very scarce, and Danny set traps up all over to supply them with guinea fowl and rabbits. But it was not going too well. Christina's clothes were haggard, so was Hettie's. They had planted some of the seed, but Danny knew well that there wasn't enough for them to survive on. Lots of farmers had turned to begging and doing small jobs all over to support their small families. Some had returned to nothing. Their families had been taken away and died in the camps. Children were few. A very young nation that loses twenty-five thousand children loses a generation and would struggle for years to get back on its feet.

She had come to him one evening. Her softness and tenderness was like a dream like falling free thru the air. Danny never got there with her that first night and felt horrible, but she wanted nothing of it. "You've been thru a dreadful war. You've seen and done things that would make many people go crazy. Most of all, this moment for both of us was so intense that it was the best ever. Believe me you being in me and being with me, I dreamed about it and thought that it would be gone forever and now it's real and it's wonderful. You'll see in no time we will be back into it. It was great, erotic, and wonderful."

As he sat there, smoking the last bit of tobacco from his pipe, he knew what had to be done if they were to survive. Danny had blanked the idea out of his head for more than a year, but he knew. Looking at Christina and Hettie, he swore.

"Shit."

"What's wrong?" Christina said.

"Listen, I am going into town tomorrow will be back late in the afternoon, then we will talk."

Mr. Cohen was a small little Jewish man with wire-rimmed glasses and with hair that came out from under a Kippah on he's head

He had one of the general stores in town.

Singers Post was a typical Free State town. It had a large Sandstone church and spire that could be seen from miles around. A post office, police station, bank, and Mr. Cohen's general dealer, the other general dealer in town, was owned by Mr. Pistorious. Hank Pistorious made his money by siding with the British during the war, carted supplies for them, was an interpreter for them, and when the war ended was well remunerated by them. He set up the small store in town. Everybody knew that Hank was sly, underhanded, and dishonest. Would not care to take every penny from those who had nothing.

Danny looked at the two stores and went over to Mr. Cohen's.

"Good morning there. What can we help you with?" Davit Cohen said.

The store was shelf on shelf of boxes and small bins. On the floor were bins with flour, corn, and sugar. A glass counter had candy jars, and inside the counter was a small arrangement of watches knives, rings, and necklaces.

"Could I see you for a moment in private please, Mr. Cohen?" Danny asked.

"Sure, sure, step in my office over here. Rachel, bring me and Mr. ?"

"Danny Venter."

"Mr. Venter, some coffee please."

Davit closed the door, and they sat down, with him behind a big desk and Danny opposite on a chair.

"I need to ask you to help me."

"In what way, Mr. Venter?"

"Well, it's difficult, but I need some money to fix my farm and to take a trip to the diamond fields in Kimberly."

"Mr. Venter, would love to help you, but you must understand I can't just lend money to anybody. I would be out of business in no time. Maybe you should try the bank."

"I know, Mr. Cohen, I know, but let me show you."

Danny took out his pocket knife and then pried open the protruding point at the bottom of his pipe.

Two diamonds rolled out.

"No, Danny, no, I don't do IDB, can't. That against the law."

(Illicit diamond Buying)

"Yes, I know, Mr. Cohen, but I was thinking this could be collateral for the loan."

Davit smiled, looked at Danny, and said, "You sure you are not Jewish?"

"Let me see. Maybe I could help."

Taking a magnifying glass from his drawer, he asked, "May I?"

"Sure."

He looked at the two diamonds.

"Well, I am not a diamond merchant, and I am not too sure of the value, but if I was to give you say thirty pounds on each diamond."

With money in his pocket and a wagon load of goods on its way to Klein Bakawaanstad, Danny walked over to Hank's store.

Hank was the only supplier of ammunition and arms in the district.

This store was nothing like Davit's store.

It was in disarray, and it would only take a few minutes to see the rat droppings and even a rat scouring amongst the jumble of stuff that stood everywhere.

He stood at the counter, a red cheeked tub of a man with shiny skin, came over.

"What can I do for you?" he asked.

No introduction, No how are you.

"Well, I need a rifle."

"Then you've come to the right place. I have Mausers and Lee Enfield .303s."

Danny pondered for a minute then said, "Let's look at the .303."

"Good choice."

"This is a Lee Enfield .303, has a magazine that takes ten bullets. It is accurate to over a thousand yards bolt action. Here let me take out the bolt so you can see."

Looking down the barrel, Danny could see the crisp cut of the rifle bore.

"Now this is a very special deal," Hank said.

"What you hold in your hand, I will sell to you for as little as two pounds, 1 and 6. To add to that, will give you one box of bullets."

"That is a good deal," Danny said. "This gun for that price plus the bullets."

"I have had a bad reputation as you know, and I try and help the Burgers when I can."

"Two pounds, 1 and 6."

As you have it in your hand.

If it's too good to be true, it's not true. Something is wrong. There is a catch somewhere That's what his boss down in Pietermaritzburg had told him.

A man standing close by walked over.

"Arnoldus," he said as he introduced himself to Danny.

"Danny."

"Did you say two pounds, 1 and 6, plus bullets? Wow."

"As he has it in his hand," Hank said.

A light went on in Danny's head. He knew what was going on.

"I tell you what," Danny said. "Give me a box of Webbly .45 bullets as well and we can do it."

Hanks stood there for a moment then said, "Okay, shake on it."

"I would like a Martini-Henry and bullets for it," Arnoldus said.

"You guys drive a hard bargain," Hank said, then smiled, walked off, came back with the ammunition and the Martini-Henry.

"Here, you take a good look," he said to him.

"Wait, let me take the bolt out so you can look down the barrel and see that all is well."

"So, gentlemen, just so we are clear. The two rifles as you have them plus the ammunition for two pounds, 1 and 6 each, and no return whatsoever. Are we good?"

"Don't want you changing your mind down the line now. Let's shake on that." They shook hands.

Danny took out the two pounds, 1 and 6, gave it to Hank, so did the other man.

"Thanks."

"The man took his rifle and ammunition, then said, "I nearly forgot the bolt.

"No, no," Hank smiled. We shook on what you had in your hand, sir. If you want the bolt for the rifle, that would cost you fifteen pounds."

"Fifteen pounds, are you crazy? How you can sell a rifle without a bolt? You robbed us."

"No, no, sir, you cannot say that. I asked more than once, 'are you happy with what you have in your hand and you agreed.'"

"The gun is useless without the bolt. You're a thief."

"Now calm down or I will call the constable."

Danny had said nothing when he saw Hank place the bolts well out of reach and behind him. He knew what was happening.

Danny smiled at Hank and said, "Good doing business with you, sir."

"Where you going with that rifle? You can't do anything with it, you know there's no bolt," he gloated.

"I fully aware, Hank," Danny said.

"Will buy it back, give you a half-crown for it."

The other man exploded.

"You Rooineck hands upper, you bastard. You caught us, and you are stealing our money."

Those Boers that laid down their weapons without a fight were called hands uppers.

Danny took the man by the arm. Very loudly, he said, "Tell you what. What's your name again?"

"Arnoldus."

"Tell you what, Arnoldus, you bring a Impala (buck) to my farm at Klein Bakawaan Stad about twenty-five miles out of town toward Bethlehem, and I will give you a bolt."

The man looked at Danny.

"You'll pay fifteen pounds for me to get a bolt, and then all you want is an Impala?"

"Never said I would buy one," Danny said loud again.

"As it happens, when we gave back our rifles at Vereeniging, most Boers wanted to break them. All I did was remove the bolts, have two of them in my saddlebag, one .303, one Martini Henry."

"You lie."

"No, come see."

"Thanks, Hank, what a bargain, man."

The two walked out the store; Hank came flying out after them.

Danny opened his saddlebag and in an old oil cloth, there were two bolts.

"Here, you can have this one," he said to Arnoldus.

"You can't do that," Hank said. "It's illegal."

"No, it was illegal to keep your rifle after the war. Nothing illegal about keeping the bolts. We have witness that, saw you sell us these rifles *as we held them without bolts for 2 pound 1 and 6*."

Then both men laughed.

Hank had just been swindled by himself. He was cross and fuming, swore legal action, but he knew he had just been done in."

A wagon load full of items arrived at the farm, and Christina and Hettie were perplexed.

"What's this?" she asked.

"A delivery from the Cohen store items bought by Mr. Venter."

"Dammit, if Danny went and made a debt, I will kill him, so help me."

Amongst the items were a few dresses for Christina and Hettie even though they were slightly large.

When Danny arrived back, Christina demanded answers.

"Danny Venter, if you have racked up a load of debt, you might as well take all this back. You hear me, right now!"

"No debt. Come, I will tell you and then you know."

He told her most of the story but far from the whole story. Never mentioned the diamond find. Just said he had found some diamonds on his way back from Hopetown.

"The diamonds were just lying on the ground, just like that."

"You lie, Danny."

"May God strike me down. I picked the diamonds up of the ground. They were just lying there. Honest."

He knew that this was only a short-term solution. He would have to go to Hopetown and get his diamonds so that Christina and Hettie could live properly.

CHAPTER 3

The cold winter morning air bit into Danny's flesh as he rode into the small town of Hopetown. He had no idea how he was going to go about getting to the diamonds that he knew were there.

He had left the farm and explained to Christina that he had to go. Gave her as little information as possible yet trying to stick to the truth.

"There are more diamonds, Christina I have seen them. We don't have to live like this. We can live an easier life."

Reluctantly she let him go.

He had a mere fifteen pounds with him, the revolver, and some supplies.

The claims office was a small building right next to the hotel. It had obviously seen better days and was not in use much at the moment.

Maps lined the walls showing the claims and their numbers.

"Can I help you, sir?" the clerk asked.

"Yes," Danny said.

"There is a farm about ten miles outside of town on the road to Cape Town. How do I go about getting a claim for that area? Want to try my luck out there."

"The Willemse farm, that's been derelict for years. Sure you want to try out there. Guys tried out in the river over there, but except for some measly small, one-half carat low-grade diamonds, nothing was found. There is no water out there to wash the dirt, and it's like working in hell with the heat even during the winter. The farm is actually for sale, has been for years. If you wanted to buy it, just shoot over to the lands office in the bank. They will help you. It might be a better option that way the whole farm is yours to look for diamonds on."

"O yes, the Willemse farm has been empty. What is it, seven years now? No water, no diamonds, nothing out there. We have been trying to sell that for ages."

"What were you asking for it?" Danny asked.

"O well, let's see. Because it is actually not of much use, we wanted fifty pounds for the complete farm. It has been a problem for us and has been on our books and we can't get rid of it. Let me tell, you Mr. Venter, that is 470 Morgen of sheer nothing (approx four hundred hectares).

It is a thin stretch of land. God knows who surveyed it, but it runs from this road leading to Strydenburg to this road that is the road between Hopetown and Prieska."

"What you asking?"

"Mr. Venter, if you carry the transfer fees and the duties, we will sell it to you for thirty pounds. All said and done, you'd be doing us a favor. It is worthless actually, but because it forms part of the town, we can't just ignore it. There might be some outstanding land taxes though. I can tell you the town council would be happy to know that someone owns it and that they don't have to deal with it. There is a big farm bordering it. We have tried to sell this place to the owner, but he said he would rather buy some rocks. He wouldn't even take it for free. He says it's so bad."

Fifteen pounds. That's what he had in his pocket, fifteen pounds.

"If I could put down fifteen pounds now, can I pay the other fifteen pounds by say, next week, Friday?"

"Sure," the manager said without hesitation.

"Can I look at the deeds and documents then please?"

"It's all here."

Paging thru every piece of paper, he found what he wanted. The document stated that the owner had all the mineral rights to the property as well.

"What if I do find water, would that increase the value?"

"To be honest sir, no."

"Seems in order," Danny said.

"Just one thing, sir."

"You can't sell it for ten years. Once it's yours, it's yours. When you sign the papers, it's your land, your responsibility, you understand that?"

He slept that night in the ruin. He was in the canyon as day broke. Frost lay thick on the ground and that meant that the snakes were in hiding somewhere warmer than the open cold air where they would die.

The immensity of what was here dawned on him as he started looking around and finding diamonds everywhere. He even dug a hole with a spade he found at the ruin, to see how deep it went. With a small cache, he made his way back to town.

"I have some diamonds I wish to sell."

"Were did you get them?"

"Out on the old Willemse farm."

"Haven't seen any diamonds come from there in ages."

"Seems they looked in the wrong places," Danny said, "or someone salted that one worked out claim" as he took out a few small one carat stones that really were not that great.

"You have a claim number?"

"No, I own the property and the mineral rights."

"You bought the old farm?"

"You're crazy man. There is nothing out her. These diamonds are a lucky find."

When he paid the bank the fifteen pounds, Danny felt relieved and walked into the pub next door and ordered a beer. The bar was empty. It was late afternoon, and the sun was just going down.

The bar was small, as was the hotel only had six rooms. The building was a flat structure. Everything was at ground level. No second floor. Swing doors led to a very small bar counter with shelves behind it and a big mirror. Empty shelves greeted Danny. The floor was dusty, a few chairs stood to one side, a side door led to a small dining room that doubled as a lounge. There were no pictures on the walls, just faded wallpaper. The barman was a skinny guy with skin like leather and watery eyes.

"Would like a cold beer if that was possible."

It was cool but not cold but still tasted great. He had not had one in many years.

"Where you from?"

"The Free State."

"Passing thru."

"Sort of."

The man with the bowler hat that came in looked very mean and strong.

"We need the three best rooms you have for tonight."

"Under whose name would that be and how would you be paying?"

The man hissed. It is for Mr. Epenheimer, Mr. Byte, and Mr. Werner. There car broke down, and they need to stay here till they can get another one here from Kimberly."

The barman's eyes went big on hearing the names, and he jumped to help.

"Sure, sure, sir, right this way."

"The gentleman would like to have some cold beer in the lounge, and then they will be having dinner before retiring to their rooms," the man said.

"We will have their rooms inspected and cleaned and ready, sir," the barman replied.

When the barman returned, he was out of breath.

"Holy cow," he said, "had to make sure those rooms were perfect."

"Told the cook to put on a leg of lamb and scoured the town for the best veggies I could get."

"Why?" Danny asked.

"Why? Because sir those gentleman sitting in the lounge own most of the diamond mines in Africa if not the world. They are probably the richest men in the world."

"They do?" Danny said and smiled.

The mean-looking man stopped Danny as he wanted to enter the lounge.

"Were you going?"

"To the lounge."

"No, you're not."

"Yes, I am," Danny said.

"Sir, there is a private function going on in the lounge and you can't go in."

The barrel of Danny's webbly was pointing at the man's belly.

"Now you're going to walk with me to their table after I have said what I want to say. I will leave. No one will be hurt unless someone does something stupid. Let's go."

The mean man was steaming with anger.

"Good evening, gentlemen, my name is Danny Venter, and I would like to inquire if the three of you would like to buy my diamond claim."

"Sorry, sir, he pulled a gun on me wasn't much I could do."

"What the hell," Werener said. "We don't go about buying claims. We are barons, we own mines, not claims."

"I know but thought you'd like to consider mine."

"A man with a gun is not someone we would want to do business with. We don't do business with thugs."

"To show I mean no harm, I will put my gun away."

Then the mean man wanted to grab Danny and throw him out, but Danny knew what was coming and stepped back.

"Will leave in one second. You don't have to throw me out. But allow me to give each of you a diamond from my claim and then I will be gone."

Danny put his hand in his pocket and then took out three diamonds and threw one at each baron. Turned around and left.

Byte dropped his Eppenheimer, just caught his, and Werner was juggling his to get control and not drop it.

"What the hell?" They stood there, each with a diamond that was at least ten carats in size.

"It can't be real. It's glass."

Eppneheimer took a small magnifying glass from his breast pocket and examined the diamond.

"It's bloody real."

"Let me see," Byte said. Werner did the same and shook their head in disbelief.

"Who the hell gives out ten carat diamonds?"

They turned, but Danny was gone.

They shouted at the mean man.

"Were did that man go?"

"He went out the front door, sir."

"Find him and bring him back."

Doubling back around the back of the hotel, Danny entered the back door, waited a few minutes, then went to the pub and sat there to drink his second beer.

Pandemonium was raging in the street as everybody was looking for him outside.

Byte was the first back. He saw Danny at the bar and nearly ran to him.

"Byte," he said holding out his hand.

"You weren't that friendly a few moments ago, called me a thug."

Werener and Eppneheimer joined him.

"Eppenheimer."

"Werner."

"Danny Venter. How do you do?"

"This claim you have, where is it?"

"O dear," Danny said.

"Can't tell you, but I will tell you what we will do. Let's go and have dinner and then we can work things out."

"Is dinner ready?" the mean man asked.

"Give me another thirty minutes, gentleman" the barman replied. "Why not have a glass of good cape wine while you wait? Then I can do the final preparation for the meal."

The lamb and potatoes were excellent. The wine was superb, and dessert were koeksiters and melktert (a custard tart and some sweat treats similar to Chinese bowties).

"Okay now, I need your guard here to leave and make sure no one comes in."

"Then we talk."

"The way I see things is that tonight about nine, the three of you will be leaving the front door with the guard who will get you some form of transport and you will be traveling to Kimberly. That's what everybody will see."

"By now most of the town knows you're here. If you were suddenly to leave with a strange man, questions will be asked and people would want to follow to find out where you guys were going."

"So your guard will get some stand-ins here in town that will look like you and will be going North to Kimberly by wagon. The real three of you will leave by the back door one at a time, walk straight out into the veld out of the lights where I will have some horses waiting. Then we will go in the dark to my claim"

"Will that work"?

"How can we trust you?"

Beit and Werner were not really in favor.

Danny turned to them, and then he produced from his pocket diamond that was not one carat less than a hundred carats.

"Please to God don't tell me that's real?" Eppenheimer was shaking as he looked thru his magnifying glass. "Holy mother it is."

Danny slowly took it from his hand, then said, "So 9:00 p.m. in the back by the veldt, okay?."

Using some old Boer tactics, Danny had them confused as to whether they were going southeast, north, or west.

It was cold, and a cold wind was cutting in to their flesh. They pulled their cloaks close to them as they went into the night. The ground crunched and crackled as they frost broke where the horses trod.

They entered the canyon

"Be careful, gentleman, this pace crawls with puff adders they are hiding from the cold, so don't turn any rocks or stones by hand. Use a stick or something, okay. Once inside I will make a fire then we can wait for daybreak."

The frost obscured the actual magnitude of what was surrounding them.

Danny said nothing. They all just sat there. He waited. By 10:00 a.m., a warm sun had made its way into the bowl and they could now feel the heat.

"How long is this going to take?" Werner asked.

"How long is what going to take?"

"For you to show us the claim?"

"This is it." They looked around, disappointed.

"This?"

"Yes."

"Have you been fooling us? here, there no diggings there, is nothing here."

"Gentleman," Danny said.

That's not frost on the rocks and on the ground. That's diamonds.

It went silent as the men, one by one, went to look and then it exploded into noisy screaming and chattering.

"Watch for the snakes, gentlemen, please."

Danny let them be for more than two hours.

"Okay, guys, we need to get something worked out."

"I have here a document that we all will sign, and there is no choice. I will shoot any person that doesn't sign. This document states that whoever tries to reveal this location and what is here to anybody will lose everything he owns, even his family, and I mean that to the letter.

"It also says that you would give me 25 percent in each of your companies. I will be a silent member of your board and will receive a salary every month equal to 80 percent of what you each pay yourselves.

"This will be paid into a bank account that you will set up for me, and the money will be there no later than the day after tomorrow. The farm, and this place, it's on, will be transferred to a farmer called Mr. Danny Puffadder. It will be owned by the four of us. The three of you will make sure that no one comes on the property, and it will be an exploration site for old artifacts. A house will be restored and occupied by people that will have only one duty to guard this farm. Each of us will be allowed to take ten diamonds from here before we leave. I will erect a gate tomorrow, and it will have four locks. Each of us will have a key. Only time we come here is when we are all present. To flood the market with this amount of diamonds will kill it.

A well will be drilled outside to give water to the wild animals

"But as I did with you, I am sure you will have no problem convincing your board members of the significance and enormity of the reserve we have here."

The silence was loud.

Eppenheimer took the paper and then before he signed asked one question.

"How deep down does it go?"

"Over behind that rock. Go, look."

He stood up and walked over to where Danny had dug a hole about twenty-five feet deep into the ground, and it was still filled with diamonds.

He signed. Byte followed.

Werner was skeptical. I know I must sign but sure would like to know more of what we have here.

"Hell, Werner, can't you see?"

He was going to answer; but Eppneheimer stood up, held out his hand to Danny, and give me the gun.

"I will shoot him right now. No ways in God's heaven is he leaving here alive. If he doesn't sign."

Werner signed.

It had taken Danny nearly two weeks to get to Hopetown. Now it took him a few days by truck and train to get home.

He was about three miles out of town when he told the driver of the truck to stop "Here is fine. Let's get my horses off."

He rode into town wearing the same clothes he left with as though nothing happened.

"Good morning," Mr. Venter Cohen said.

"Good morning, Davit."

"And what can we do for you today?"

"Let's talk in the office," Danny said.

"We have a problem?"

"Rachel, coffee for me and, Mr. Venter."

"Please call me Danny."

"So what is it today, Danny?"

"Well, Mr. Cohen, when I needed help, you gave me help. You saved me."

"No, Danny, was just business, that's all."

"Well, I am here to pay you back."

"So soon you must have done well on the diamond fields, Danny?"

"I think I did, Mr. Cohen."

"Davit, call me, Davit."

"Here." Danny took out one thousand pounds.

"What's this?" Davit said. "It's way more than the money. I gave you way, way, more."

"I know," Danny said.

"Can't take it."

"You have to."

"No, no."

"Please," Danny said, "just take it."

"Danny, it's way too much."

"And," said Danny, "and this is absolutely legal."

"I want you to take the two diamonds. I gave you and give one to Rachel and one to Miriam. Have a nice necklace or ring made for them."

Davit had no words.

"Danny, no one has ever done something for me ever or for my family, why?"

"Because, Davit, you're honest and you helped a Boer in need. Enough said."

"This is between me and you, okay? I'm just Danny from a farm outside town."

As Danny was about to leave, it was Rachel who stopped him.

"Danny, would you be so kind as to send your wife and daughter into town to the store. We just got in some lovely woman's wear and clothes. Dainty stuff, you know?"

"Will do, thanks," Danny said.

He bought himself a small buggy from the livery and a lovely new horse. His old trusted horse would be put out to pasture, some more supplies for the farm.

As he was about to leave, he stopped at Hank's store.

He walked in. Hank came out from behind the counter.

"You're not welcome in my store. I want you to leave."

Danny stood there and looked at him. Then he grabbed him by the shirt.

Hank gasped for air.

"Marta call the constable quickly."

Danny didn't let go.

"You will make sure that every farmer you did in with your famous special gun deal gets all their money back. You will never ever as much as steal a farthing from anybody. If you do, I will close you down and you will never, ever, ever be able to work anywhere in South Africa, if not Africa."

Hank was breathing hard.

"Who do you think you are?" Hank was brave as the constable arrived.

The constable walked in and drew his revolver.

"Let Hank go, sir."

"No problem."

"Constable, I want you to send this telegram at the post office to the minister of police. Mr. Rogers then tell him to contact Mr. Epenheimer, the diamond baron, and tell him you've locked up Danny Venter for telling a man to stop stealing from the public."

"Don't think I can do that."

Danny turned to the constable. "So let's go to the post office, and I will do it."

"You can't do that, Constable. This man threatened me with bodily harm. He did. I have witnesses."

"Constable, if you don't send the telegram and Mr. Rogers finds out you've locked me up, things could really look bad for you."

The young constable put the revolver in its holster and then said. "Think this was a big miss understanding no harm done", turned around, and left.

"Constable, come back," Hank shouted.

Danny looked at Hank, and he could feel the heat at the back of his neck. He was so cross.

"Wait here."

"Will not," Hank said and went inside his shop.

"Philip Aldridge was the bank manager when Danny walked in. Aldridge was in his office, so the bank teller asked if he could help.

The bank was a sturdy sandstone building that looked more like a courthouse than a bank. Big brass bars separated the tellers form the clients. The walls were white with the occasional portrait of some bank board members. Visible thru the bars was the door to an office where a man sat looking at some papers.

"Yes," Danny said, "that's the manager over there?" "Yes."

"Tell him that Danny Venter is here."

"The manager is very busy, sir, would you like to make an appointment to see him?"

"Just do as I ask if you want to still work here by the end of the day." Danny was in no mood for this, was still upset with Hank.

The manager nearly fell as he came out the office. "Mr. Venter, please to meet you. We had a wire from Johannesburg that you'd be in your accounts, have been set up as you asked. "Please come in, please."

The manager had him sign some documents, asked Danny if he would like some coffee or tea.

"Is there anything else we can do for you, sir?" he asked.

"No one will know about my account and the money I have. Is that clear? The only person that deals with my account is you."

"Two things: make sure my farm is paid off, second thing, come with me."

They crossed the street to Hank's store. Hank was back inside still ranting about what Danny had said.

"Hank, meet Mr. Aldridge, the bank manager."

"Mr. Aldridge. Please explain to Mr. Pistorious over here that if he doesn't do as I told him to do, he better start packing and quick. As you will financial ruin him and that you have the power to do it. One farmer comes and complains one, he's done."

Danny turned and walked off.

Hank went white after Aldridge had spoken to him then he sat down then started shaking. By the time Aldridge left, he was a walking corpse.

Only thing Danny ever told Christina is that he had a good find on the diamond field. He also told her she could get whatever she needed, asked her not to be extravagant, as he didn't want any attention.

"By the way, Mrs. Cohen wants you and Hettie to come over tomorrow, something about women's dainties that arrived form Johannesburg."

The news came by the constable. Danny had to go to Johannesburg. Byte had died, and the board required him there as the son was about to take over. Danny new exactly what it was all about. The son would have to be informed, taken to the site, and shown.

"Sorry, Christina, but this is important. I really have to go, and I will be away probably for two weeks."

"Can't someone else go?."

"There is trouble at my diamond mine."

"Hate it when you're not here."

She wasn't happy at all, but if Danny said it was important, she could believe that it was.

Two days later;

Someone called her by her surname, Mrs. Venter, in a singing tone. She wiped her hands on her apron and then went out the front door, on to her front porch.

Donald Black stood there in his evil splendor.

The same feeling she had in the camp, the fear, the hate all came flooding back.

"Get off my farm," she said.

"Well, now, Mrs. Venter, see that's not very kind."

"Get off, or my husband will make sure your are off feet first."

"Now, Mrs. Venter, we know your husband is away, and we heard he will not be back for a while, so now, now."

"Just get off my farm please."

"Well, would like to, ma'am, but we have some unfinished business, you and me."

Christina looked at him, and she could feel the anger welling inside her. *Not now*, she said to herself, *not now*.

Where was Hettie? was all she could think of.

"Well if you will be so kind, Mrs. Venter, see way over there by the willow tree. The willow tree was a good 250 yards away. That's my friend, Patrick Peal. You remember him well, don't you? And standing next to him on that little barrel is your lovely daughter. She looks so good. Mmmm . . . can't wait to know her better."

"You touch my daughter, and I will kill you with my bare hands, you pig."

Christina was scared, very, very scared. She had no idea what to do; fear was driving her mad."

"Now you might not see it from here, but I have a rope around her neck tied to a branch above her head. My friend Patrick is tied to the barrel. If he falls down, he will yank the barrel from under her, and she will die before you can get to her.

So if you were to shoot me, he would just yank the barrel out and be off, and she will die. If you shoot him, he will fall over and yank the barrel, and she will die. Good plan. Hey, don't you think so?"

Fear turned to anger and despair all the same time. They had planned this perfectly, and there was nothing she could do.

"Now knowing all that don't you think we should put our differences aside and get down to some serious stuff, why don't you just get undressed, save me the effort, and I can have a good look at your body before I help myself to it."

Christina went blind hot angry. She struggled on what she was going to do, allow him to rape her, and then Hettie. What was she going to do? Rather than have that happen, she would shoot her own child and herself. She struggled squinting into the house and found the rifle. Had a hard time making sure it had three rounds in the magazine, then as she slid one into the chamber, she went outside.

Donald Black was enjoying himself. "Hope you're getting undressed, my dear. Can't wait all day. Sun is getting hot. My friend, Patrick, can't wait for his turn, and then we are going to have turns with Hettie, and who knows do it all again just for old time sakes.

She came outside with rifle in hand, squinting.

"Now, now, Mrs. Venter, you shoot me, your Daughter will be dead. You know that, so put away the rifle. Come, it will not be that bad. I will be gentle."

Still squinting, she walked right up to him. He had his hand slightly raised. She made sure he stood between her and Hettie. She grabbed him by the neck, shoved the rifle, point into chest, and pulled the trigger. The sound was muffled by his body, and by his clothes, she used all her strength to keep him standing.

"O shit," Hettie said as she turned to Patrick. "My mom's gone white, you're dead."

Patrick had heard the muffled shot but wasn't sure what it was. He saw Donald standing there with Christina He turned to talk to Hettie.

"What are you talking about?"

Christina looked at the tree that seems a mere twenty yards away. She saw Patrick turn to talk to Hettie. In that split second, she dropped Donald and shouldered the rifle. The fear made her unsteady as she saw her daughter look straight at her as she looked down the barrel and the sites of the rifle. Tears flowed from her eyes. She fired.

Donald dropped to the ground.

There was this ripping sound like someone ripping paper; then, Patrick saw the rope slowly like in slow motion snake down and fall on Hettie's head.

As he turned to the direction of the sound that followed, the bullet tore into his chest from the side and out. He was dead before he hit the ground, yanking the barrel form under Hettie.

All she feared was that Hettie was dead.

Christina ran as fast as he could, falling as she couldn't see properly, screaming Hettie's name.

As she came closer, she saw Hettie struggling to her feet, her hands still tied behind her back then lay in to the dead Patrick with her shoes.

"You pig, you made me fall, you shit."

Christina struggled the last few yards and grabbed Hettie in her arms then she broke down and cried.

Six months earlier

Within a week, people arrived to repair and fix the house, tin roof, proper door windows, a pump in the kitchen for water, a lovely outhouse, and a big stove. New furniture.

It was while the men were fixing the roof that it happened. The big hammer caught Christina a glancing blow on the head and knock her out. When she came to, she was lying in bed with Danny and Hettie big-eyed looking at her

"Are you okay?"

"Think so," Christina said. "I'm feeling a bit dizzy and my head hurts, but I seem to be okay."

"Bloody idiot just left the hammer on the tin roof and it slid off."

"Hope you didn't fire him."

"Yes, I did."

"Danny, it was just a mistake. Bring the man back. Let him finish the house. He's doing a wonderful job."

"Hettie, go, stop that man walking up the path. Tell him to come back."

Christina's pride and joy were her chickens—all eight of them. She fed them, got eggs from them, and when the chicks came made sure they were well fed and that the hawks did not catch them.

Saturday afternoons, Danny would take Hettie and show her how to shoot with the .303. She was good but not wonderful. Did not take long for Christina to join in. She wanted to know how to use a rifle to defend herself. If the likes of Breton Winslow were ever going to come this way, she wanted to be ready. Danny showed her, and soon it ended up in a competition, which Danny won every time, even when shooting left-handed. Christina had listened to Danny on how to breathe and aim, the front site being in the vee of the back site, the point level with the site. How the increments worked on the back site.

She loved it, and soon Danny had his hands full as Christina became quite a good shot.

The commotion outside at the chicken pen made Christina rush to the back door. It was a barn-type door. She saw the little jackal run of with one of her prize chickens in its mouth.

She went white-hot and furiously cross. But as she turned to get the rifle, things seemed very strange. The house seemed out of shape, the items seemed closer and bigger. She struggled to get hold of the gun but was determined to get that damn Jackal. She pulled the bolt back, and the bullet slid in the chamber.

She stumbled to the back door, and she looked outside in the direction. The jackal had run. It seemed strange the veldt was closer. She saw him standing there with the chicken still flapping in its mouth. Shouldering the rifle, she took aim, and things were bigger than usual, very big and the jackal very close. "Didn't even think to run away, you little shit," she said, aiming for the spot just above his front legs, breathing properly, squeezing instead of pulling, and then she shot. The jackal made a back flip, and the chicken flew in the air.

"Hettie!" Hettie came running around the front of the house.

"What you shooting, Mom?"

"That damn jackal tried to steal one of my chickens, so I shot him."

"What's wrong with your eyes, mom? They look scary, and you look pale."

"I'm okay. just go, get my chicken"

"Where?

"Over there," Christina said. "By that big rock."

Hettie looked out at the field.

"What rock?"

"Over there."

"Just next to that old tree."

"Can't see it, Mom."

"Dammit, Hettie, just go there, that way you will see it."

Hettie shrugged her shoulders, and she went off. Two of the farm black children who she had been playing with followed her.

It was only when they had covered the first one hundred yards that they saw the tree and then the rock. They ran the last seventy yards and found the dead jackal. One of the black kids found the chicken close by looking a bit bedraggled.

Hettie turned and looked back at the farmhouse. It looked small from where she was standing.

How did Mom shoot this jackal that far? she wondered.

She shook her head. *How did mom see the jackal, much less shoot it at this distance perfect heart shot at that?*

Hettie called it mom goes white. Danny asked her one day what she meant by that.

"Well, Dad, when mom's eyes go all black and she will go all pale and white. She can see for miles. I lost her little spoon once near the gate. She went white then shouted at me to bring it back, and I was frantic, couldn't find it. She walked from the house to there, see there where the road takes that sort of bend, see where that big tuft of grass is next to the road. She came from the house all the way over there and picked it up out off the grass. Gave me a big hiding can tell you that."

Danny asked Christina about it.

"I don't know, Danny, it's when I get cross. It's like my eyes become binoculars. I can see stuff miles off but struggle close by having to squint to make sense of what's close by, else I walk and bump into everything. Strange, but no harm though, do feel dizzy when it happens. But else, I am okay."

Danny had just got back to Hopetown after a secret mission to their "mine" with Byte Eppenheimer, Werner, and him signing a new document. The constable shouted at him, "Mr. Venter, Mr. Venter, big trouble on your farm. All we know is that there was a shooting, and two people are dead. Will try and get some more information."

Danny feared the worst. He had lost his wife and daughter. Guilt tore into him. He should never ever have left the farm. The constable had no idea who got killed. All he knew was that there were two people.

It's amazing what money can do. Danny stood in the engineer's cabin of the train as it sped thru stations one after the other on its way to Arlington station where they had fresh horses waiting to carry him to the town.

It took him just over twenty-four hours to reach the town, covered in sooth, and smelling like coal and steam. He was met outside of town by Mr. Cohen.

He arrived just as the sun was rising.

———

"Where is Christina and Hettie?"

"Danny, they are safe. They have both of them in jail, but they are unharmed. Rachel made sure they were warm and was well looked after."

Danny burst into the police station.

"Who the fucken hell locked up my wife?"

The constable and sergeant jumped back in surprise. "Mr. Venter, sir, we have no options. She had shot two men on the farm. We have to, till we know what happened."

"Let her out now," Danny said.

"Can't do it, sir. She's in there under suspicion of murder."

"So help me, Sergeant."

"Now, Danny, they are okay, they are safe. These men are only doing their duty. Come, the sergeant will let you see them. The magistrate will be here tomorrow with the traveling court and all will be sorted out," Cohen said.

Danny tried to stay calm as best as he could as they took him to see Christina and Hettie.

"How the hell do you lock up a child?"

"She went mad. She would not go anywhere else, wanted to stay with her mother."

They hugged and cried, and then Christina told him what happened.

"Now what happens?" Danny asked the sergeant.

"Well, the judge and the state lawyers will come in and then hear what she has to say and determine if she stands trial for murder."

"And who talks for her?"

"We don't have lawyer for her."

"That would be the bloody day."

"I don't care the cost or what language you use but I need this message to get to Mr. Eppenheimer right now highest form of urgency, I will be waiting for the reply."

It took a mere twenty minutes for the reply to come back, much more formal.

Lawyers dispatched. Stop will be in town by twelve noon. Stop traveling thru the night. Stop best lawyers in Jo burg stop.

There wasn't even a witness to say they had seen her fire the shot and the fact that Hettie claimed that her mom had shot the rope blew the whole case apart and due to lack of reliable witness or evidence, both were set free.

Two days later, a constable from Bethlehem had come to town to visit his mother, and when he heard about what had happen told the sergeant that two men were wanted for the rape of a woman outside of Bethlehem. It turned out to be Donald and Peel by the descriptions.

Danny made sure the farm was fenced and employed a guard at the gate to make sure no one came on to the property.

All would have been over and done with if it wasn't for Hank. He just couldn't let go. He had to make fun of Christina wherever he could about how she could possibly think that anybody would have believed she shot the rope in the tree at 250 yards.

He hated the Venter's, hated Danny, and if this was a way of getting back, he was going to use it.

"She had help," he always said. "She had to have been helped by someone. Maybe a lover who knows."

Nachtmaal (communion) is a big gathering in any Boer town. From all about farmers and their children would come to town camp there to partake in communion. It was a festival. With dancing and cooking and competitions, even the prize horse, cow, and bull would be chosen. The festival lasted more than a week.

As Christina sat there with Rachel and Miriam, her daughter, they spoke about the new dresses that were expected to come in and the perfumes that they occasionally got.

He was slightly drunk, and his breath had the smell of cheap home brew peach brandy.

"Now, Mrs. Venter," Hank said with a slur.

"The men have a shooting competition over there as you can hear. And I told them they are no good at what they are doing, the best shot is Christina Venter."

"You're drunk, Hank, go away."

"Well, I told them," he carried on, "any person that can shoot a rope at 250 yards must be an amazing shot or lying. What you say?"

It was like she was hearing Breton Winslow with he's sarcasm and evil wit.

Christina had not gone white in ages. But she was there in a microsecond. Her eyes all black, her face pale; she stood up.

"Let's go see," she said in a voice that would make water turn to ice.

"O shit," Hettie said and made all the ladies spill there tea.

"Dad, dad, dad!" she shouted as she went looking for Danny.

Christina struggled to walk.

"Rachel, could you please help me to the shooting range where the men are?"

"Are you okay, Christina, you look pale?"

"I am okay, just take me to where they are shooting."

"You don't have to do this, Christina."

"I have to."

"Are you all right? Your eyes are all big and black. Do you want to sit down? You look like a ghost, you are so pale."

"I'm okay," the voice was still like ice.

As she reached the place where the men were shooting, Danny came at a brisk pace and walked up to her.

"What's going on?"

"Its Hank. He's been at her again," Rachel said.

"Where is the bastard? I will kill him."

"It's nothing," Christina said in that cold voice. Her big black eyes looking at Danny.

"You have nothing to prove, Christina, nothing."

She wasn't listening at all. She was cross as could be. She had just been called a liar in public, and he was going to apologize.

"Give me the .303," she said to Danny. "Make sure there are three bullets in the magazine."

"He shrugged his shoulders, and a few seconds later returned with the rifle."

"I need 4 half-crowns."

"Don't think I have. I have two."

"Here," Rachel said, "I have two."

"Thanks will give them back to you later."

Hank was beckoned over

"Hank, want you to go with the constable out there at about two hundred yards, there is an anthill. Place one of the coins on the hill for me. Then just another twenty-five yards back there is an old tree place one there, and then there is that old gate post, place one on it please."

Hank was going to protest, but when he saw the look in Danny's eyes, he listened to what she said.

"The other coin, you can just place here with that target that is at fifty yards and everybody can have a go at it once I am done."

"You're joking," Hanks said in a surly voice.

"If I miss, then I would be a liar, wouldn't I, Mr. Pistorious?"

The two men walked out to the anthill. Everybody that had any binocular or spyglass was looking out at them.

Hank smiled back at everybody, waved elaborately at them with great care, placed the first coin on the anthill, then he stood up to walk away when the coin flew off in a blur flowed by the noise of the rifle.

He jumped back. "She nearly hit me," he said to the constable.

"Don't think so. She hit the coin though," he replied.

"Holy Mary."

The men were all talking and pointing.

The next time he placed a coin, she didn't give him much space before shooting it. By this time he was a nervous wreck. He couldn't place the last coin. His hand was shaking, and he couldn't place it on the post.

The constable did but made sure he was between her and the coin. Once he had it secure he just fell on the ground and the coin disappeared a second later.

The men had all been watching with telescopes and binoculars.

In an instant, the shooting range was like an auction, people were shooting and screaming.

Rachel smiled at Christina, "I knew you were a good shot, but that was some shooting. I always said to Davit she shot the rope, he had doubts. Typical man."

No one, not even Danny could shoot the coin that was placed at fifty yards, no one could.

After everybody had tried and Christina calmed down, Danny took Hank by his shirt neck, lifted him up, then dragged him on to a wagon.

"Hank here has something he would like us all to hear."

"I do," Hank stuttered.

"Yes."

"I don't know what I must say."

"Let's see. Don't you think you've been lying to everybody and that you owe my wife an apology?"

Hank stuttered thru his little apology, and when done, Danny threw him from the wagon.

"You piece of shit," he said, "I want you packed and out of town by tomorrow afternoon. Then he turned to the local *dominie* (pastor), "Sorry," he said.

The pastor smiled and said, "Couldn't have said it better myself." Everybody laughed.

Christina stood there looking out toward where she had shot the coins. A small boy and a girl were looking to find the coins. She was calm now. They had been there for more than two hours. It reminded her of the orphan kids in the camp looking for food, and her heart went out to them.

"Hettie, come here,"

"Tell the boy the coin is just behind the rock next to the small anthill. Tell the girl the one coin is over to the left in that big tuft of grass, as for the last coin it actually flew back toward me, hit the back of the anthill straight inline between me and the post."

The coins were where, she said they would, be. The two kids, showed them proudly to everybody. They were from the poor part of town, and it touched Christina's heart.

"Danny."

"Yes, want you to buy back the coins from the kids. They are special coins, so they have gone up substantially in value Think three pounds should be a fair price for the three."

The kid's mom was elated and thankful. Danny cradled the coins in his hand, each were shot absolutely perfectly in the center. He looked at Christina and shook his head.

CHAPTER 4

Christina realized she had lived a secluded life on the farm and that she had everything she wanted. Needed for nothing, but there were people struggling in town that had a hard go of it. They were people that were victims of a very bad war.

She wanted to help, to do something, to take away the pain and hurt the camps had brought.

Going to town with the buggy she took Walter with her Walter was the guard. She called in at Rachel and explained what she had in mind.

It didn't take long before she had a woman's group that made it a point of seeing that all children in town—black or white—were fed, that they had a place to sleep and went to school. She made sure that parents—men and—women were given opportunities to work at whatever work they could do to reestablish themselves. Every time she went to Danny saying, "I know you're not going to like this, but I need more money if I want to help these people."

Danny would say, "I'm sure we will find some money to help. How much do you need?" Christina was way ahead of her time. She excelled. She was doing good. She was mending hearts and minds. But in her heart she had a hate that was driving her wild making her sad. Christina could not mend herself.

It was always there: the fear, the anger, the bitterness. Breton Winslow. He had done indescribable deeds yet was never ever asked to account. The Bloemfontein cemetery at the camp cried out for him to be brought to justice, but he was never ever found.

Sometimes she thought she had seen him in the street, but it turned out to be someone else.

But it was always there, always haunting her. That same fear and anger she had when she saw Donald and Patrick and the same hatred that made her pull the trigger without a moment of guilt and the fact that she actually enjoyed shooting them was locked in her mind. Nobody knew, not even Danny.

The dairy outside town was the property of Adrian and Santie Brink. They had a daughter, Gloria Brink. From an early age, Gloria had been a tall girl big, in stature, perfectly shaped body, but a big girl. When the school year started and Hettie had to go to school for the first time, she was happy until everybody stared mocking her about her red hair.

When she tried to defend herself, the kids ganged up on her.

As two girls and a boy was pushing Hettie down on the ground calling her names, one boy thought he just sprouted wings. Gloria took him by the scruff of his neck and threw him one side the girls followed Onlookers didn't wait around a scurried off to cover. She helped Hettie up. My name is Gloria. Kids mocked me because I am big. "Me and you we will make a good team."

They were inseparable, Hettie and Gloria.

Gloria worked and lived on the dairy farm with her mom and dad. Her father had no squabbles by having her do work that boys would have to do on a farm. Her mother on the other hand tried her utmost to raise Gloria as a lady.

Rachel and Christina were sitting in her house that was in the street just behind the shop having tea.

"I need to be able to help the poor people in town. Lots of them had been thru hell in the concentration camps, and they surely didn't need to suffer any longer."

"I know, Christina, I feel the same way. It's just like when we try and help, people sometimes misuse you. You know."

"I know, but even so, those that don't are worth the effort."

"There this young boy outside of town by the Liebenberg's. Think his name is Tommy.

"They have a really bad broken piano, and he would sit for hours trying to get some tune from it. He has such a passion to want to play, but he can't because there is no one to show him and then there is that broken piano. I know if I was to ask Danny to buy one for me, he would probably say yes, but I don't think it's right. It's like I would misuse his kindness."

"Well, Christina, I think I can help out with one of the problems. Come with me."

There was a big shed next the house, a place to keep wagons and the bigger stuff that Davit could not keep in the store: old trunks saddles, ropes hanging from the roof, planks, boxes with nails, an ox wagon, spades, forks, sheets of glass.

"Watch where you walk, lots of old nails about."

At the back of the shed in a corner stood a big box covered with a tarp.

She took the tarp off, and there was big crate.

"There."

"What there, what's this?"

"In this box is a piano, brand-new, never been played ever."

"What? You lie?"

"Yes, was bought for the Silberstein's when her husband was the town doctor."

She died, he didn't want it, and it has been stored here forever."

"You're lying."

"No, my dear, it's there, weighs a ton, and I just know that Davit would gladly have someone take it off he's hands."

"What you think he would want for it?"

"Forget what he wants. It's what I want."

"That is?"

"I want my Miriam to play."

"Miriam to learn piano?"

"Yes."

"So if I can get a teacher to teach the kids piano, you'd let her have the piano thru me, but she has to teach Miriam for free?"

"Sounds like a good deal to me." Rachel held out her hand.

Christina shook Rachel's hand. "Deal."

Weeks went by without as much as a sign that anybody could help with piano lessons. The church organist said maybe, but she really doesn't play piano, only organ. Some leads just ended up in a dead-end, someone playing a prank on someone else.

"Santie, I just don't know what I am going to do. I am at my wit's end. I have a problem, and no one can help me," Christina said as she drank her coffee.

The front porch to Santie's farm looked out on a big meadow where a dozen or more black-and-white cows were eating lush green grass.

"Well, Christina, sometimes problems are easy to solve. Other times they need some help, and sometimes you just can't do anything."

"I know, but I really feel this one is a dead-end."

"Well, you know, if you were to tell me the problem, who knows maybe, just maybe, I could see if I can give advice and help."

"Well, Rachel has this piano she will give me if I can find a teacher to teach Miriam how to play. I want the piano, so I can help Tommy to play. But I have looked and asked everybody in town, and no one can help, not even Petronela, the organist can help. So I am stuck."

Santie took a deep breath then said, "What I see is that you need someone that went to a music school in Cape Town or maybe Durban who is a certified pianist? Someone who has played some concerts, maybe, someone that has grown up with music. Her father was a conductor, her mother a violinist. Sort of thing."

"Come on, Santie, that would be perfect, but were on God's earth do we find someone like that in this town?"

Santie started laughing so much she had tears in her eyes.

"What's o funny?" Santie asked.

"Just sit here I will be back."

"Here have a look."

The big binder was full of photos, concerts, and a person playing piano. In it was a certificate that read as follows. To Santeria Columbine, honor's degree in music from Cape Town University.

"This isn't you. No way, this is you? Come, don't play games. This is not you."

Santie stood up, bowed, and said, "I present Santeria Columbine Piano virtuoso."

"No, you're lying, Santie. No."

"I am Santeria Columbine. My father was Richard Columbine, conductor of the Cape Town Symphony Orchestra. My mother Eleanor Columbine, first violinist of the same orchestra."

Christina had no words. She just sat there her jaw hanging open.

"Say something?"

"Can't. I am speechless."

"Will I fit the, job Mrs. Venter? Is my credentials in order?"

"You'd do it? You'd teach?"

"Would love to. Have not touched a piano in, what, five years? Like good wine to a dry soul would love to play again."

Arrangements were made, and it was decided to bring the piano to Santie's farm. She would place it in her lounge and then the kids would be brought there to have music lessons.

It never stayed at just Miriam and Tommy. Very quickly it became a half-dozen pupils. Santie was in heaven to teach these kids; to play was just fantastic.

At night she'd sit there by herself and just play the Handel's the Bach's, Mozart's, and Hayden's to her heart's content for hours. Gloria and Adrian Would just sit and listen. Gloria was mesmerized by the way her mom's fingers jumped over the keys.

Miriam was a good student but not wonderful, did enough to make her mom proud. But it quickly surfaced that she longed to play violin. Davit made that happen; Santie was not wonderful on the violin but was good enough to teach basics.

Tommy was excellent, played with his heart, and would never ever miss a class and would come hours before the time to practice.

Very seldom would one come to the dairy farm and not hear music.

As Santie was watering her roses in the garden, she heard music. Must be Tommy, she thought. But then she realized that the music being played was not Tommy's music. It was way too advanced. No, this was a Bach piano concerto being played by someone that was amazingly good. She put down her watering bucket and walked to the lounge. So as not to disturb the player, she slowly went inside.

"Gloria," she said aloud.

"Sorry, Mom. I thought you'd gone to town, sorry." Gloria had been told to stay away from the piano and never touch it. Gloria stood up, and it was obvious she was close to crying. "Did not mean to, Mom, sorry. Honest."

"Gloria, who showed you how to play?"

"I'm sorry, mom, will not do it again."

"No, it's okay. Mom's not cross, don't worry."

"Who showed you how to play?"

"No one. I just listened. When you showed Tommy and Miriam."

"You listened, so you play because you've heard."

"Yes, and I look at the music."

"What music?"

"This music."

Santie took the sheet from Gloria's hand. It was one of her Bach Concertos, a very difficult piece to play at the best of time.

"You read this, and you play it?"

"Yes."

"This?"

"Come, sit down here, and play this again for me."

Accept for two very small mistakes, Gloria played the whole piece flawless.

Santie was just about in tears. She had her own daughter sitting and listening while other kids were taught by her and her own daughter was brilliant if not amazing at music, and she never ever knew.

"Can you play this one? She took out a sheet of music by Mozart."

"Yes," and she did. This time, no mistakes.

"And this."

"And this."

"And this."

Gloria played every piece of music her mother could produce.

"Gloria, listen to me, listen to Mom. Whenever you want to play, you play, okay? You can come here and play on this piano any day, anytime."

"You sure, Mom?" Gloria said with a big smile.

"Yes," she replied with tears flowing like rain form her eyes. She grabbed Gloria and held her against her chest. "Mommy loves you."

She couldn't believe that her daughter had this amazing gift.

When Christina came over for tea that Monday, she couldn't wait to tell her . . .

"You will not believe what happened come, come, sit down."

"I will show you."

"Gloria," she called.

"Gloria, can you play for Mrs. Venter, please."

Gloria faltered and then shrunk back.

"No, Mom, I can't play for her."

"Come, come, child, you can, you know you can."

She sat down, and it was a disaster. She missed notes and made mistakes everywhere. It really sounded awful.

"Sorry, Mrs. Venter," Santie said. She walked over to Gloria. The child was on the verge of tears. "I am to scared if there are people," she said.

"Okay, okay, maybe we will play some other day, okay?"

"Tell you what, me and Mrs. Venter will go sit outside and have some tea. You practice some Hayden."

"Okay."

Once on the porch, the whole farm was filled with music: pure, excellent, faultless music.

"The kid's amazing." Christina said.

"Isn't she? Never taught her a thing. She listened and taught herself while I was teaching Tommy and Miriam. And the other kids."

"Does seem like she's very frightened of playing in front of strangers."

"Seems like that. She might just be nervous. You're her first audience. We will have to work on that," Santie said.

Gloria and Hettie were above-average students. Hard workers. When the time came, they went to boarding school together in Kroonstad to finish their high school. They were fortunate many students went to work the farms after the completed primary school.

Gloria never ever played at school. She just couldn't; she would fall apart.

Tommy was sponsored by the Venters and did very well at the high school.

By the time Hettie and Gloria graduated from grade twelve. Gloria was a woman of six foot and three inches tall. She towered above all the other girls. She wasn't overweight, wasn't out of proportion, a very perfectly shaped body but just very, very tall.

During school holidays, Gloria would work on the farm with her dad. It didn't take long for the suitors to arrive and see if they could woo over this girl. At sixteen years of age, most farm girls would have been married already and have maybe one or two kids.

Adrian didn't help much; when the suitors arrived, he would let them work with him and Gloria. It soon dawned on them that she was one strong woman. Seeing her lift bales of hay, logs and big pieces of iron made them back off.

At first, Gloria didn't think much of it, but she quickly caught on.

Picking up a full can of cream weighing about eighty pounds was not the easiest of feats.

She did this just about every day and never thought much of it.

She would take the can by both ears, and then she would lift it up in front of her and carry it to the house for her mom. Most men would struggle, to lift a can, much less carry it. Usually that would be their last visit. They never seem to come back. The dad laughed, but Gloria hated it. It made her feel like some sideshow and a freak.

Danny had to get bore holes drilled, and so he contacted the mining people in Johannesburg, and they send down a drill operator. He drilled a bore hole for water, so Danny could feed the cattle and have good water on the farm.

To help other farmers, Danny used his influence, telling the board members that it might make good sense to drill some holes all over to make sure there weren't any coal or gold deposits that their competitors might find. He actually just had the drill operator drill all over on every farm so the farmers could have water and not pay to have a bore hole drilled.

Sergey Dalnov was a big man a huge man. He was seven foot four inches, tall, a giant of a man, and not an inch of a fat, all muscle.

He had come to South Africa by boat from Russia.

"In Russia we don't ask what we want to do, we get told what to do by the Tzar," he would say.

"So I worked in the mines and then they put me on surface drilling to drill to see if there was gold ore."

"I got tired and then one day just started walking south ended up at the Black Sea. Then got on a ship, ended up in Cape Town, just before the war. They used me to drill holes for the military so they could have water on the way to the north. After the war I purchased the borehole machine and became a contractor for the mining companies."

Adrian was amazed by this tall man and his strange accent when he spoke Dutch.

As they sat on the back porch, Gloria was playing some Tchaikovsky. Sergey loved it.

"Tchaikovsky," he said to Adrian, "very good Russian music."

When she finished the piece Santie called out.

"Gloria, can you bring the cream cans to the kitchen for me?"

Gloria had no idea that there was someone with her dad. Neither did her mother.

She walked out of the house without a glance toward Adrian and Sergey.

Sergey just caught a glimpse of her before she entered the room next to the stable.

She looked very tall for a woman, he thought.

As she came out the separator room with the can, a big man came at a brisk pace toward her.

Sergey watched this wonderful black hair tall woman walk across the yard a few moments ago.

Then she came out the room next to the stable carrying a big can.

Before Adrian could utter a word, Sergey was off the porch walking briskly toward her.

"No, no, no," he was saying, "you can't carry that. Let me help put it down."

Never ever in her life had Gloria looked up to a man.

She had to turn her head back to see him.

Sergey was a handsome Russian man, brown hair, no beard with large golden flecked green eyes.

"Give to me," he said you can't carry that. "No, no, no."

Gloria was speechless.

She just stood there dazed. Gently like someone taking a baby from a mother, he took the big can in one hand, and without any effort at all flung it over on his shoulder. Where do you want it?" he said.

Gloria stuttered then bewildered said, "The kitchen it's got to go to the kitchen. I will get the other can."

"No, no," Sergey said again, "let me." He went inside the separator room and came out carrying the other can in the other hand over his other shoulder.

Gloria was astonished and totally smitten.

His green eyes seemed to look right into her soul as to know each and every one of her thoughts. She blushed. First time ever in her life.

The two people came walking to the kitchen.

"You played the piano, you play good."

"Thanks."

"Like Tchaikovsky love his music."

"I like it too."

He stopped at the kitchen door, lowered the cans, and then stooped to go in, carried the cans into the kitchen where Santie was standing. She dropped a big pan on the ground when she saw him. Adrian emerged from the side door.

"Ladies, want you to meet Sergey. He's the drill contractor who is going to drill some holes on the farm to look for gold and stuff.

"Sergey, my wife Santie and my daughter, Gloria."

He held out an enormous hand; its touch was gentle like a butterfly on skin although worn and calloused from years of working.

Gloria was still bloodred blushing.

Santie saw it said nothing to her but smiled. "Sergey, would you like to stay for dinner? I have a lovely side of beef. I am cooking."

"Would be wonderful, ma'am, but I need to set up camp, get my drill equipment, organized, and ready for tomorrow. Maybe next time, but thanks you very much, smells wonderful."

Sergey had seen many woman in his life, but this was an amazing woman. Tall, very tall, to what he had seen in his life. She reached his shoulder, and most woman could easy walk right under his arm. Had jet-black hair and the most amazing blue eyes he had ever seen. When she looked at him, he felt like he was drowning, like it was hard to breath. Never ever had that happened to him in his life.

They sat there and enjoyed the evening meal. The talk was about this giant of a man and how strange it was to see someone that tall and strong.

"He just flung those cans on his back as though he was carrying a small bag of potatoes," Adrian said.

"Saw you blush first time ever," her mother said with a big smile.

"Come on, Mom, come on."

When they finished off without a word, Gloria dished up a big plate of food and then walked out into the night. "What's that about?" Adrian said.

"It's for Sergey. She's got it bad for him can tell bad." Santie smiled.

"She can't go out there by herself with a strange man."

"She is, and you're not going to stop her," Santie said looking at her husband that made it quite clear.

Sergey sat at the fire he had made. He had his drill rig behind him. He had suspended a tarp to give some cover and made sure his oxen were looked after. As he sat there drinking some coffee, all he could think of was those amazing blue eyes of Gloria.

Something stirred in the night. "Anybody there?" he said. "It's me, Gloria. I thought I would bring you some food." Sergey jumped up spilling coffee all over himself.

"Gloria?"

"Yes?"

"Come, come."

She entered the light; he took the plate form her.

"Sit her in my chair."

He tried not to show that his hand was shaking, so he put down the plate on the small table.

"I just brought the food," she lied. "Have to get back."

"Please stay," he said, "let me finish the food. You can take the plate back. Then I will walk back with you and you can take the plate back."

She tried to hide her approval by looking back at the farmhouse about seventy yards away.

"I really should go."

"Please I don't want to eat this lovely meal alone."

There was an awkward silence for a while until he spoke again.

"My whole life people stare at me, made me feel like I was a monster. Like I belonged in a circus or something. I always had to show how strong I was or do some stupid things to amuse people. That's why drilling is such a good job for me. I am out here in the open by myself. No one staring at me, can just be me."

"I know how it feels. I also was stared at, laughed at, made fun of, called names because I am so tall. Some kids used to call me a heaven broom, said I am so tall my hair sweep the bottom of heaven."

It was with a start that Gloria realized that she had been sitting, talking to Sergey for more than two hours. "Man, Dad is going to kill me. I really have to go."

She jumped up.

"Come. I walk with you."

When they reached the house, her father was standing at the kitchen door.

He was going to speak, but it was Sergey that spoke first.

"Mr. Brink, I apologize for keeping your daughter. I asked her to stay till I finished my food, and it has been all my fault. I am a very slow eater."

Santie appeared. "Was the food good?" She smiled at Sergey. "Wonderful and delicious. Haven't had such a good meal ever honest."

She grabbed Adrian's arm as he was about to say something.

"No harm done, Sergey. Thanks for seeing her back safe."

Adrian felt her vice like grip on his arm, and he knew whatever he was to say next could be big trouble for him.

"Don't think anybody would have dared harm her with someone like you around. Have a good evening."

"Thank you, Mr. Brink, Mrs. Brink."

"Goodnight Gloria"

He left into the night.

Adrian was about to fly into Gloria, but one look from Santie said it all.

"I'm going to turn in," he said. "Good night, Gloria."

"Good night, Dad." She was amazed her dad had not said anything about her being out there with a man for two hours.

"So, so, so. Come, lady, talk, talk."

"What, Mom?"

"Tell me everything."

"Mom."

"Tell, tell."

They sat there having some tea and Gloria without knowing was telling her mom she just met the man of her dreams. She spoke about him in such loving terms without even knowing she was doing it. She told her mom about his background about Russia.

Gloria had a hard time sleeping that night, the thought of being with him in an intimate way was eating her alive. Never ever had she thought about a man in that way. She felt guilty and prayed to God for forgiveness for having such thoughts. The thoughts did not go away; actually they became stronger.

After four weeks of drilling, Sergey had left to the next farm, every evening he would come by sometimes traveling as much as fifteen miles just to see her for a brief moment.

It had to come, and Sergey asked Adrian if he could have his daughter's hand in marriage.

"Would gladly say yes, Sergey, you're the ideal man and would be the ideal husband for her. But I need to ask you to wait. I want Gloria to go study at university. Want her to get educated and become someone, not just a housewife. So I will allow you to get engaged, but you can only marry once she finishes university."

Gloria was not happy with that arrangement. Neither was Santi, but Adrian stood firm.

"No, will not back off on this. Sorry, it's this or nothing," he said to Gloria.

"Dammit, Dad, that means I have to wait for him for four years."

"Yes."

"Four years?"

"If he loves you, he will wait for seven like Jacob in the Bible for Rachel."

"Dad!"

"No, that's the final answer. It's this or nothing."

They got engaged on the farm; the Venters and most of Santi's students and dairy customers were there. Miriam played, and her mom was so proud.

"Why don't you play?" Sergey asked.

"Can't, Sergey, I fall apart when there's people.

"I just can't." She had played for him many a day without any problem, but with strangers, she just couldn't.

"Okay, one day," he said and left it at that.

For Hettie, life was life. She seemed to get thru life easily. Things that would phase others just seemed to be nothing for her to handle. She was an amazing debater and did very well at all the debate competitions she entered.

But as for boys, it was just not there. She never found a boy that made her feel tingly and special and warm. It didn't really worry her, and she never entertained it.

The camps had made her hard. She always feared that whoever she cared for or loved would die like her friends in the camp.

The university College of Johannesburg situated on the north side of Johannesburg established by the mine consortium's in Kimberly years before was the primary seat for higher education north of Cape Town.

Sunnyside Res was where Hettie and Gloria were residing.

Hettie was allocated a bursary in studying Law while Gloria was going to study Music.

Hettie would find it easy to study. Gloria had no problems either except for one detail, the practical. She feared it and hated it and knew she would, as always, fall apart.

But Hettie had found a solution and asked her professors to allow Gloria to play in the big hall while they would sit way back where they couldn't be seen at all.

It work amazingly well, and Gloria did extremely well, passed her practical exams with accolades.

Samantha Smithe, the daughter of one of the mine managers, was in plain words a spoiled bitch.

She ran everybody down. She humiliated everybody and expected everybody to be at her beck and call. Her father was the mine manager of the biggest gold mine on the Witwatersrand, and she made sure everybody knew that, Gloria being big and Hettie having her blood red hair were prime targets for her constant remarks about being stupid farm girls and their appearances were a source of fun everyday. She and her friends would play dirty tricks on Hettie and Gloria, bringing them into trouble with the faculty.

Hettie being quick to figure things out made short work of these games. As she would see them coming, she would side step them or have them backfire on Samantha and her friends.

Gloria in her own way would do things to them that they didn't even think of being possible.

She would carry all their furniture downstairs, place it in the foyer or outside at night when they were away for the weekend.

They never thought that a girl could be that strong to do all this, and the men would be blamed much to Gloria's delight.

The final year had come. This was it for Gloria. This was fantastic. As soon as she was to receive her graduation certificate, she and Sergey were to marry. She studied hard and worked hard. The Saturday after the graduation ceremonies, she and Sergey would be married. Not a week later.

The break for the September holidays was surely needed by all, and Hettie and Gloria stepped off the train at Arlington station. Sergey was there with his big truck, and Hettie and Gloria laughed as they bounced along in the front of the truck sharing the front seat.

"Typical farm girls," Hettie said holding her hand at an acute angle.

"Typical," Gloria replied, and they both laughed.

Being home with family and friends is something money can't buy. It's just so good.

Sergey and Gloria spent every day out at his rig. Wherever he was drilling, she made him food, washed his clothes. Needles to say, they went as far as they could without doing the deed, the shame, and ridicule of a girl pregnant and not married, was something, which would kill both her mom and dad.

The wedding was not to be.

War had come, a big world war, the war to end all wars. Due to Danny's standing in the commercial world, he was never required to go.

Sergey was drafted not to war but to work in the supplies stores in Pretoria. He never did go to war.

Then the war ended, and everybody was happy. The world could breathe again. Many did not return, many died, and battles like DELVILLE wood claimed a lot of young men.

Sergey would try and get to the farm where Gloria was, whenever he got some leave.

They got married that summer in January 1919. A typical farm wedding Christina and Danny stood in as parents for Sergey.

Now it was over, and everybody was trying to be as happy as could be.

Hettie was at home just lazing about and would take long rides on her horse. She longed badly for something, but she had no idea what she was longing for.

Sat for hours under a tree somewhere feeling terribly lonely, even cried sometimes.

What is it I want? she asked herself, but there was never an answer.

"Well, ladies, we have a situation."

"I have been asked to attend the annual Mine magnate's ball in Johannesburg at the Grand Station hotel."

"You have what in heaven's sake for, Danny?"

"Beats me," he said.

"Mr. Venter, his wife, and daughter are cordially invited to attend the annual mine magnate's ball in Jonnanesburg at the Grand Station hotel at 7:00 pm on Saturday, the 14 of February 1919."

"That sounds wonderful," Christina said. "Don't know what one wears to such an occasion, but I am sure Rachel can help. You don't seem very thrilled, young lady."

"Will be okay, Mom, but I have no one to go with, and then I have to sit with you and Dad like a spinster. Everybody will be looking. I will feel awful. Why don't you and Dad go? I will just stay home."

"Sorry, Hettie" that will not happen Christina said.

Gloria and Sergey pulled up outside.

"Hi, hi."

She told Gloria about the ball.

"You must go, sounds absolutely amazing. Who knows you might meet a handsome guy? You just have to go, Hettie."

"I don't think I want to."

"What? Wish it was me. Would die to go to one of those fancy balls."

Danny stood up and excused himself.

"Your dad doesn't seem to happy that you don't want to go."

"I know," Hettie said, "but it will be terrible with all the old people and just me."

Danny returned a few moments later. "I love this new phone thing," he said.

"Okay, they can go, but they will have to sit at the back."

"What? Hettie said. "What?"

"Gloria and Sergey, they can go, but they will have a table at the back."

"Mr. Venter, are you sure?"

"Yes, yes, you travel with us, stay in the hotel with us, all will be taken care of, will even make sure you three ladies have the right evening wear. As for Sergey here, well, I will take care of him."

Christina took Danny's arm and spoke to him on one side.

"Danny, we can't do this. It will cost a fortune."

"Don't worry, my love, it will be okay. I have a large nest egg I can use."

With that, he turned around and said to Sergey, "Come, let's go have a walk and smoke a pipe."

"That's wonderful. Love you, Dad." She gave Danny a big hug.

Clothes were a big concern for everybody. Formal, absolutely formal.

For Christina, Hettie, and Danny not such a big problem, but for Gloria and Sergey, a major problem.

"No problem. No, no problem. Here you go to this address, and, Christina, Hettie Gloria, you go to this address. My friends in Johannesburg will help you. No problem—everything, shoes, gloves, and hats, coattails—everything you see."

Davit smiled.

Isaac Levy had a tailor shop just of Ellof street in Johannesburg.

The store had two large display windows both with manikins in full dress suits, top hat, and tails. Inside the store were rows and rows of bolts of material. On one side, suede leather shoes were display at the bottom on top of the shelving were some hats. A faint smell of leather hung in the air. The two men entered, and Isaac stepped back.

"I was told to expect two gentlemen, one a large man, very tall. You must be Sergey, and you must be Daniel." He used the proper Hebrew name, not Danny. "Davit told me you'd be around. So we have this big formal ball at the Grand and you gentleman have to attend."

"Let's start with you Daniel. I think a size 40 would be just right for you. Let's just measure and make sure." He took a tape from his shoulder, measured Danny's arms, legs, collar, waist, etc.

"Mmm 40 would be just fine. A size 9, say 10 shoe, and let's see, a large hat, size 7 1/8. Yes, that's it, perfect. A 17 collar, no problem, as for you sir. Now, we do have to do this as a special."

"Sergey was quiet up to now. Your name again Sergey. Russian, you said?"

"Lots of Jews in Russia."

"Now allow me just one moment. I have a friend in the back room that always complains that I never give him something extraordinary to make. Always the same stuff he says, Isaac. always the same stuff."

"Benjamin, I need you to measure a customer for me."

"Isaac, I am busy back here. Can't you do it?"

"Would gladly if you don't want a special job," he said and winked at Sergey.

There was a shuffle movement at the back of the store then a short bald headed little man came out. He stopped and looked at Sergey. Then he smiled. "*God* is *good*," he said. "At last something that would get my brain some exercise. Wonderful." He smiled with a big broad smile.

With every measurement he made for Sergey, he would repeat it to Isaac. "That's right. Arms at the top by the biceps, 28 inches in diameter, yes, 28."

"Size 10 hat, maybe a bit bigger."

"Shoes, o my goodness, shoes." Both men stood there and looked at the boots Sergey was wearing. "Shoes?" Then looking at each other said at the same time, "Ishmael."

"Levi," they called. A young man came in the store form the back. He stood there mesmerized by Sergey's size. "You go down to Ishmael. You say the following exact words. My dad says you need to come to his store. He needs the best cobbler in the whole of South Africa. For a very, very special job. That's all, you tell him nothing else."

Although they were sworn enemies, one Muslim and one Jewish, when it came to business, they were the best of friends.

"While we wait for Ishmael, why don't we have some tea or coffee?"

A young girl entered carrying a tray. Sergey stood up and took the tray from her just before she could drop it." Don't stare, Sara," the father said.

They had just finished the coffee when Levi returned with a Muslim man in his full Muslim regalia, long one-piece gown in pale blue. A fez on his head, the typical Muslim beard and dark black eyes looking out from a very dark skin.

He stopped as Sergey stood up again. "Goliath," he said.

"What you know about Goliath?" Isaac said.

"I know more about your religion than you know about mine, Isaac. How are you?"

They laughed.

"This is my dilemma, a pair of dress shoes to match the coat and tails we are making for this man."

"Now I see why you said you need the best cobbler. That's me of course. Shoes for this man. No problem, we make him the best shoes ever."

"May I borrow your tape please, take off the boot please," he said to Sergey.

"Mmm . . . yes, that seems a bit big. Let me measure again. Yes, yes."

"Okay have enough here to make him shoes that will fit him like soft slippers."

Isaac said, "One small issue."

"What?"

"Need it by Friday. A week from now"

"This Friday?"

"no next Friday"

Ishmael rubbed his beard and then smiled. "Friday one week from now at twelve, okay?"

"Perfect."

He laughed.

"May I make as second pair just to display in my store, sir?" he asked Sergey.

Sergey looked at Danny. Danny shrugged his shoulders. "Sure."

Sergey turned to Danny when they left. "Mr. Venter, I appreciate all this. but I honestly will not be able to afford this."

"You will not. It's on me."

Danny held up his finger. "On me," he said.

"Haven't been able to go shopping for anything with a man and that felt great not having to look at woman wearing this shoe and that hat and that."

"Will pay you back," Sergey said. "You already did. All the bore holes you've done for me is payment over and over again."

"Let's find a pub and have some beer."

Agatha's woman's fashion store just off Market Street was one of the most renowned ladies stores in Johannesburg. Only for the rich and wealthy.

It had a high ceiling soft lights and a long row of fitting booths all with lights and curtains.

In the middle of the store was a big circular bench were the ladies could sit and watch those trying on clothes.

Dresses were long, straight, no belt or middle, mostly shoulder straps, tight-fitting semi-high heels. hair tight to the head with a cap like hat, feathers, and long stringy jewelry, and of course long gloves all the way past the elbow, and a cigarette holder about fifteen inches in length even if you don't smoke.

The three women entered and was greeted by An Lebowitz. She held her hand to her mouth.

"O my goodness," she said, "sorry but I have never ever had someone of your stature been in our store," she said to Gloria. "This is a good day for us. We always say we can clothe any lady and you are it, my dear." She laughed and held her hand out to Gloria.

"An . . ."

"Gloria."

"An . . ."

"Hettie."

"An . . ."

"Christina."

"Come some tea for you while we decide what we want to wear?"

Gloria came up to Christina.

"Mrs. Venter, I don't think I can afford this?"

"I know you can't, but Danny can. His exact words were 'buy whatever you need. I will take care of the bill, that's for everybody, Gloria as well.'"

"You sure?" Gloria said.

"Absolutely sure."

"Now, ladies, the two of you. We have a large arrangement of designs and fashion. We will let you look at and try on."

"But as for you, my dear, you're a special project. Let me just go get our seamstress Rosa."

She returned a moment later with a lady on her arm.

"Our seamstress."

Gloria stood up towering a good one foot over the seamstress.

She wasn't shocked. She smiled look at An and said, "Now this here is a woman, lovely, beautiful, amazing like Venus de Milo. Now this Italian lady will show you all what a dress looks like."

"Come with me, young lady, we have work to do." With Gloria on her arm, they disappeared in to the back.

"I have to ask you not to be modest but want you to strip down completely, have to get your exact measurement."

Gloria stood there all six three of her naked. Rosa held her hand to her mouth. "Perfect, absolutely perfect. You are magnificent, my child. Your husband sure is a lucky man. O my god, you are amazing."

"Sorry, sorry, let's measure."

Taking careful notes, checking and double-checking till she was sure she had Gloria measured. "Get dressed, my dear. Now let's see what will we wear. Material first."

They were interrupted every few minutes to come have a look at what Christina and Hettie wanted to wear.

Hettie chose a very soft blue braided dress with beads.

Christina opted for a straight silver-colored dress, very plain, body hugging, and amazingly sexy.

"Can we get this lady sorted out?" Rosa said with her hands on her hips.

Bolts came and went; dresses were shown and were put one side.

They sat there four woman looking at Gloria. "What are we going to do?"

A small girl came in, didn't even take notice of Gloria, hugged Rosa. "How are you, Gran?"

"How is my little butterfly?" she said.

"Good. Mom told me to wait here. She's just off to the bank."

"What a grown-up girl you are becoming to come into the store by yourself. Give me a hug."

"You look worried, Grandma," she said to Rosa. "Grandma has a problem. See that lady? We want to make her a special dress, but we can't seem to find anything that would look good on her."

"Please stand."

Gloria stood up. "She's a giant, Grandma."

"Sorry," Rosa said. "We don't say that," she said to the girl.

"It's okay," Gloria smiled. "I like it when she says it. It makes me feel like something from a fairy tale."

The little girl came walked around Gloria, looked her up and down, and then went back to Rosa. "Grandma, remember you once told me people don't always know what they want and then they get things that is not what they really wanted?" "Yes." Rosa frowned, not having any idea what the child was talking about.

"Well, you bought that material for that lady she wanted for her curtains, then she said no. There is a lot of material would be enough for someone that's a giant." "Enough for a giant. You're right."

"This kid is going to be a fantastic designer, I tell you. Let me go get that material."

She returned with a paper wrapped bolt

An said, "Surely, Rosa, you can't make a dress for this young lady from curtain material?"

"Well, Ann," Rosa said, "when we ordered the lace Mrs Jones wanted for that special valentines party she wanted red. Then once it came she said no to dark and she wanted pink This is red lace."

"It went into storage and has been there for more than three years. Who is going to buy a bolt of red lace?"

Delicately Rosa started unwrapping the paper a small section of blood red lace fell out.

This was no ordinary lace; this was not curtain material. This was handmade Croatian lace, soft and gentle to the touch. perfect in every way. Expensive but very feminine.

Gloria stood up, touched the lace, and said, "O I love this. I want this. This is it."

"I know," Rosa said, "blood red for a one of a kind woman."

"We will underline it with a skin colored petticoat and it would appear that your naked underneath" she giggled.

"We have the material now, the work can begin."

They stayed in the Station hotel's most expensive rooms. "Hettie in one, Danny Christina in one, and then Sergey and Gloria in one.

They were going to be there for just over a week. Enough time to get dresses and shoes made.

Christina asked Danny. "Danny, I am worried. I know you say you have a nest egg, but this is crazy. It's going to cost a fortune. You sure we can afford this?"

"I am sure we can," Danny said. "Don't worry. It would be all okay."

A big commotion in the morning had Danny and Christina looking out their door down the passage. The manager was standing at Sergey's door. "I don't care, sir, nobody sleeps on the floor in the Grand. If the bed is too small, we will make you a bed so you can sleep like a gentleman and that's that."

Danny laughed and closed the door. Christina giggled like a naughty schoolgirl. Her nose crinkling up as she laughed.

"Come here, you woman," Danny said, grabbed her, and lay her on the bed.

"Mr. Venter," she said, are you intending to have your way with me?"

"I sure am," Danny said.

"I hoped so," she laughed again.

The mine Chambers ball was the social event of the year only surpassed by the ball in the castle in Cape Town. Anybody that was of note in society would be there.

The glamor and glitz, cameras, reporters.

The four of them came down and entered the foyer that led to the hall. They just wanted to enter the hall as any other couple would when they were stopped. "Would the Venter party please follow the bellboy to another room?" a man said. Hettie said she wasn't going with and would stay with Gloria and Sergey. But the man was adamant. "They would be taken care of and taken to their places, but the three of you have to come with me. Please. madam."

"What's going on?" Christina said.

"I don't know think they want us to meet the board members that's all. Will be okay. I know some of them," Danny said.

Christina had a feeling that something was happening, but she had no idea what.

"You'll be okay?"

"I think so," Gloria said nervously.

As Danny, Christina, and Hettie entered a private room, they were introduced to the other men and their wife. Christina and Hettie had no idea what was going on or who these people were, and just played it by ear.

After making sure where they were on the guest list, Sergey and Gloria were announced to enter.

"Mr. Sergey Dalnov and his wife Gloria!"

As they entered the ballroom, a hush of silence filled the room.

People stopped and stared.

Sergey in coat and tails filled the room with his presence and size. On his side, Gloria, in her bloodred lace dress that clung to her like it was painted on to her body made a few men stare. The flesh-colored petticoat and bra gave the illusion she was naked under the lace. Her height and amazing long legs brought gasps to many a lady and man.

They were magnificent in there stature and size. She looked comfortable next to the giant of a man. He made her look small, but she looked blood curling sexy.

He was the emperor of Russia. Walked like a man that owned the world.

They were escorted to their table.

One person was not impressed. She sat with her father. Samantha Smithe.

She sat there at her table then whispered in the boy next to hers ear, "What is that Amazon doing here?"

"I think she looks amazing," the boy said. Samatha just shrugged her shoulder.

"Amazon."

The ball was to start with a dinner; then, a recital then the actual ball.

As the last guest entered, the doorman shouted out loudly.

"Will we all rise for the entrance of the board members?"

Mr. Epenheimer and his wife, Mary
Mr. Byte and his wife, Sonja
Mr. Wernner and his wife, Olga
Mr. Venter and his wife, Christina, and daughter, Hettie

Christina tugged on Danny's arm. "A board member. You're a board member, and I don't know about this."

She squeezed his arm hard. He winced.

Samantha spilled her glass of water onto herself.

She started shivering then she felt she was going to cry then she tried to hide.

Her mother looked at her and said, "Behave yourself. Compose yourself. Don't make a spectacle."

A thousand wasps flew into Samantha's head. She had called one of the board member's daughter a common farm girl. She had humiliated her over and over again. Played dirty tricks on her. Her father would kill her if he found out what she did. Tonight she dies. It's over. *My life is over*, she thought. She was shivering like she was standing in a freezer.

Worse was to come when the managers and their families were introduced to each board member. When Samantha came to Hettie, it was her father that spoke, "You went to the university here in Johannesburg, did you not? You must know my daughter then, Samantha."

"O I do." Hettie smiled and looked Samantha straight in the eye. "Of course we were big friends. How are you, Sammy, are you well?" Samantha didn't speak; she just stood there.

Hettie squeezed her hand very hard.

After the formalities, dinner was served, waiters flew back and forth like bees feeding queen bees.

There was some small talk at the table but nothing extraordinary.

The music coordinator stood up and said, "Ladies and gentlemen. Unfortunately we don't have Mr. Edelstein available. He had just been run over by a horse and is on his way to hospital. It seems that he was not seriously hurt but would be unable to play for us tonight. So I apologize as we don't have anybody that could play the Tchaikovsky piano Concerto for us. He was about to add that they have a violinist that would play them some Mozart—" But a big giant of a man stood up and said, "We do have someone, Maestro. My wife, Gloria."

Gloria died then died again and died again.

"Please, Sergey, don't do this to me please."

She was shaking. "It's time," he said. The world should see and hear you play. "Come." He stood and very, very reluctantly, she followed him to the stage. Samantha's jaw dropped again.

"She can't play?" she said

He helped Gloria on to the stage. "It will be okay you'll see. Just do what I tell you to do."

The piano was facing the audience so they could see the person playing.

A grand piano that had taken three men to shift in position stood center stage.

"Can we turn the piano?" Sergey said. "We can, but we might need some help."

"It's okay," Sergey said, took one leg, and like moving a small chair swung the piano so Gloria sat with her back to the audience.

Then he sat Gloria down.

Sergey turned to the people who were murmuring and talking.

"Please, ladies and gentleman We need absolute silence. My wife is very nervous, so let's give her a chance."

The hall went deathly quiet.

The magnificent back of Gloria's dress low-cut showed her figure perfectly as she sat there. She was shaking.

Her black hair, short and snug against her head, with big sliver earrings hanging from her ears.

"How can you do this to me, Sergey? How could you? You know I can't do this. I will look a complete fool," she whispered.

"Now look at me, just at me."

"Gloria, look in my eyes. Nowhere else. Just here, my eyes."

"Listen the people have gone. I showed them to leave. Don't turn around. Believe me, there's no one there. I showed them to go outside and listen. If I'm lying, you never ever have to talk to me again. I've never lied to you ever."

She wanted to turn, but he took her head softly in his hands.

"Play. Play for me, play Tchaikovsky for Sergey. I will stay here, you look at me. Like on the farm—just you and me here. No one here, no one."

"Look, my eyes, okay, nowhere else. You don't need to look at the music, just my eyes."

She took a deep breath and started playing slowly at first, but Sergey stood there smiling at her nodding his head. Her fingers flowing over the notes like raindrops dancing on water.

She finished her eyes closed. It was quiet; no one was actually there. Then she jumped as the hall exploded with shouts of bravo, Hettie leading the cheers. Christina was crying, so was Hettie. Samantha also cried; this was terrible.

"More more," they shouted.

"You lied, Sergey You lied." She was cross. "I know, but listen to them. Listen, Gloria, they are applauding you."

"I never thought I was good enough," Gloria said. She was crying too. "You are." She slapped him on the arm. "You lied."

"So don't ever talk to me again."

She leaned over and gave him a kiss on the cheek.

The music director walked over. "Absolutely amazing," he said. "Wonderful."

"I have here the pieces Mr. Edelstein had selected to play if you want to have a look."

She glanced and then said, "You think I should try again?" she said to Sergey.

"Yes."

"I am not sure. They are difficult pieces, you know."

"It will be quite in order if you can't play them," the director said.

She sat down still extremely nervous.

Here my eyes. nowhere else.

She smiled and looked at him. "I need to look at the music."

"No, you don't. You know all those pieces by heart. I have heard you play them over and over."

She went from one to the next, and every piece gave her more confidence.

The music coordinator was about to say thanks when Sergey saw he had another sheet still in his hand.

The people wanted more.

"What is this?" then he took it from the music coordinator.

"Mr. Edelstein had brought this music by someone called Rachmaninnov."

"Rachmaninnov. I know the man. Big hands played like a demon."

Sergey looked at Gloria. She looked at the sheet. Her eyes went big. "Wow," she said, "this is surely an amazing piece of music."

"It is known as one of the most difficult pieces of piano music ever written," the director replied.

"Mr. Edelstein practiced for hours every day," he said. "Wished he had bigger hands like the composer to stretch for the big notes."

The audience was spellbound deadly quiet listening to every word said. Even the board members were captivated.

"See over here the director pointed to a piece of music on the page."

Gloria looked at it and then played the note effortlessly. "That's it right there," the music director smiled.

"Would you like to try?"

She looked at Sergey then shrugged her shoulders. "I don't know what do you think. You think I can do it, do you?"

Sergey just smiled and nodded.

"What the hell," she said softly.

"Ladies and gentlemen, Mrs. Gloria Dalnov is going to attempt with the permission of the board members, what is currently known as one of the most difficult pieces of piano music in the world, second only to the Bach 4 concerto that she played effortlessly. The Rachmaninnov 4 piano Concertino in D major."

Hettie stood and shouted, "Do it, Gloria, I know you can!" Then she sat down embarrassed.

Gloria shuffled herself on the chair. "Here goes," she said. But before she started, she waved the director over. "Could you just turn the pages for me? Don't want to lose concentrations."

"Surely," he said.

The music that filled the hall made even Samantha sit up. It filled the heart and soul of everybody there. The magnitude of the piece, the enormity of the notes was astounding and touched every sense of every person, sound, smell, sight, and touch, feeling the music vibrate on their skin. Her magnificent frame sitting at the piano, her hands dancing over the keys, then slow then fast, then pounding the keys that it looked like they could break.

Her dress slid to one side revealing her long muscled leg. She didn't notice, just played. This was Gloria in her own world back on the farm playing for no one but herself as a small girl.

She finished, and it was quiet. She looked big eyed at Sergey; even he had a tear in his eye. "Was that okay?" She didn't want to turn around. "Look," he said.

As she turned, everybody in the audience—men and women—had hankies drying tears from their eyes. She stood up slowly then bowed.

Even if the building had caught fire, the noise would not have surpassed the applause she got.

Someone somewhere had found a big bunch of flowers and came running up to the stage to give it to her. Gloria Dalnov had arrived, and the world had taken note.

Gloria Dalnov would be her name.

As she went to sit down, people still applauded.

The time for the address by the chairman of the board had come.

Epenhiemer stood up and took the microphone.

He was going to say something about the war but knew it would spoil the evening so didn't. This was an evening of joy, and he wanted it to stay that way.

"Seems like our friend, Danny, over there has been hiding some exceptional talent, back there in his town. Well done, Gloria."

"Ladies and gentlemen, I present to you our Board Members. These board members and our company are of the wealthiest people in the world today. The combined wealth of our company is more than some small country's total wealth. I present the world's diamond men. We are diamonds. My friend, Danny, over there is an obscure person. If you were to go see his farm Klein Bakawaan Stad, you'd see no difference to any other Free State farm. A humble man. But a generous man.

"Young men, take note, his lovely daughter had no one on her side when she came in." He laughed.

Christina glared at Danny. "The most richest men in the world. You?" "Yes," Danny said. "And I don't know, your wife, and I don't know?" She slowly pulled his head toward her. You are in such deep shit, Danny Venter. You will never ever get out of this ever."

Christina sat there. Neither she nor Hettie had any idea about this in any form or way. They just thought that Danny had found a good diamond claim and that he was getting some money from it and so they needed for nothing.

Hettie was dumbstruck. Her dad was a millionaire, and she had never ever known.

She giggled. Her eyes caught that of Samantha to one side trying to be a small as possible. She waved at her like she was a long lost friend. Samantha waved back her hand, looked like a shot duck falling from the sky.

As she turned and looked at the audience, she saw Gloria and smiled. *Wow, this is going to be amazing*, she thought.

Sergey looked at Gloria. "No wonder they paid for all this. They can easily."

Samantha fainted and had to be taken out by her boyfriend.

"Finally as this is a big event we decided as members of the board to give each lady a small gift—" waiters came in with trays with small boxes on them.

Please don't open till we ask you to.

Everybody got a small box. Samantha had returned, carried her little box in her hand. No boxes were given to any of the board members' wives or Hettie.

"You may open the gift," the chairman said. Inside each box was a small half carat diamond pendant on a sliver chain. There were oohs and aahs then a big round of applause.

"I want to invite my wife Olga to the front. The diamond I am about to give her is from a mine only, known to our board members."

He took out a box, and in it was a pendant with a pure white diamond on a chain; the only difference with her diamond was it was a good 30 carat stone.

"Thanks for your support and love." He gave her a kiss and escorted her to her chair.

The young Byte came to the microphone and said.

"I wish my late father was here tonight to see all this and enjoy this with us. I'm very poor at speeches. But no man can achieve a thing without a woman by his side. Thanks, Sonja." He gave her a similar stone of the same carat size as Epeneheimer had given Mary, his wife.

Next up was Werner.

In German, he said how he loved Olga, thanked Olga, and then gave Olga a blue diamond, smaller in size but still very spectacular. There were a few that frowned because he had spoken in German; wounds of the big war was still raw.

Danny was last. He stood there, looked at everybody for a long time, then said, "I'm just a plain farm boy form the Free State. My dad was a transport rider. I have never been much in life, and when I found one of the riches diamond caches in the world, it meant nothing to me as at that moment I wanted to be with the biggest treasure I have ever had. It's not money, it's not diamonds that bring happiness. It's having an amazing woman by my side. Would gladly without blinking an eye give every diamond I owe, every penny I have as long as I know she'd be by my side. Christina, thanks." He held out a big bloodred diamond that was a good 35 carats and hung it around her neck. He was about to leave when she held him back.

"I think he said that it takes a special kind of man to bring out the best in a woman. We saw that tonight with Sergey and Gloria. I know I speak for Mary, Olga, and Sonja when we say thanks to our husbands."

She applauded; the audience joined in and stood up.

As they walked back, she said softly, "Don't think for one moment, Danny Venter, that this diamond changes anything."

Epeneheimer came back to the microphone. "We suggest that you make sure your pendants are safe, so wear them that way you know where it is at all times."

Hettie had not received anything at all. She felt left out; nobody had noticed.

Only Gloria did.

She came over and said, "See, they never gave you a pendant. Here, take mine please." She said, "No, no, sure my dad will make it up to me."

She was still talking to Gloria when a tall young man with thick rimmed black glasses came up to her. "Hettie Venter."

"Yes?"

"My name is Arnold Zimmer. My dad is one of the lesser board members. I couldn't help but notice that you never received any pendant."

Hettie looked surprise. Someone had actually seen; someone had seen she hadn't got anything.

Then she felt that small shiver as though someone had moved her chair.

"May I give you this pendant? It's the only one I could get at short notice from the jeweler in the foyer. Had to threaten the owner with force to open the store for me this late, so please don't let my efforts be in vain."

"If you'd be so kind."

He took the pendant from the case and gently placed it on Hettie's neck.

The pendant was a smaller diamond than the ones everybody else got. It was plain and simple. It was as much as he could afford.

When he touched her, a small electric spark flew into her body, and she jumped.

"Sorry did it hurt you?"

"No, the necklace is just a bit cold," she lied.

"Sorry didn't think of that."

Christina had seen the young man and then saw him give Hettie a pendant.

It dawned on her Hettie had not received anything. She had been overlooked, a major error.

She grabbed Danny's arm. "You never got Hettie anything. Now you are even in deeper shit, Mr. Venter.

"O my god. This evening is turning into a nightmare for me," Danny cringed.

"Dammit with everything going on, I forgot."

"Well, that young man there just saved your ass. Saw him give Hettie a pendant."

Danny stood up and walked over to the young man. After giving Hettie the pendant, he had walked over to his parents and was standing there having a glass of champagne.

"Danny Venter. Arnold Zimmer Sr., my wife Petra, and my son Arnold Zimmer Jr. An honor to meet you, Mr. Venter."

"Actually the honor is mine. Mr. Zimmer, your son here is very observant and a very exceptional young man."

"Thanks, sir, can't see why."

"This young man was the only person in this entire crowd that saw that one of the most important people here never got any gift." They looked at Danny perplexed.

"My daughter. I made a huge error. Never gave my daughter a pendant. Don't know where you got that pendant, young man, but there is no way you are paying for it. How much was it?"

Arnold Zimmer Jr. looked at Danny and then said words that Danny will always remember.

"Did you not just say that you'd give anything as long as you had your wife by your side, did you not say she was special?"

"I did."

"Well, sir, I don't know Hettie at all, but to me a lady that beautiful and elegant should not be something that two gentlemen should be haggling about when it comes to a gift given in appreciation of her presence."

Danny was speechless so was Zimmer and his wife. Arnold Jr. said, "Glad to have met you," then turned and walked away.

"Don't know where you got, him people, but that there is a true thru and thru gentleman. Would like to meet him for lunch if it's all right with you."

"Sure."

"I will arrange it," Danny said. "Would like you to contact me in the morning, Mr. Zimmer. Need to know more about him. Please thank him again from me."

Needles to say, the name Arnold Zimmer was quickly on every board member's lips.

He had saved them a huge embarrassment.

Hettie sat there dumbstruck. Gloria was giggling and was just ecstatic. "Come on, Hettie, you got the best pendant here tonight. This guy, this Arnold, saw you amongst everybody and thought you were important enough, to go buy you a pendant out his own pocket. That is so romantic."

"Where is he?"

"He is talking to my dad."

"Hope my dad didn't have anything to do with it."

"No, I don't think so. You think so?"

Danny came over. "I'm sorry, Hettie. I will make it up to you. It just slipped my mind, honest. You know dad loves you very much."

Hettie looked at her dad then held out the small diamond pendant. "It's okay, Dad, I got one, Dad, a special one."

"I know. That an amazing young man that is. He saved our butts, he did. Where is he?"

"I think he left," Hettie said.

Hettie waited and looked but did not see him anywhere. She made her way to the foyer.

"Excuse me," she said, "did you see a young man with thick black-rimmed glasses? A tall man? Skinny."

"No, ma'am," the man said.

"The bellhop in the lift said, "I took him up to the roof, ma'am. He wanted to go see the city lights."

"Take me up please."

She came out at the top floor.

"The stairs are around the corner to your right."

She found the stairs, walked up one flight of stairs thru a door, and found herself on top of the world looking over the city of Johnnesburg.

She walked to the edge and looked down. Seven stories down.

"Be careful," a hand grabbed her shoulder.

It was Arnold.

"I've been up here few times when my dad stays here. Night is the best day time is a bit smokey unless the wind blows then you can see quite a distance."

"Why did you buy me that pendant?" Hettie asked.

"Because you didn't get one."

"But how come you saw and nobody else?"

"Because nobody else was looking at you. They were looking at lesser jewels."

"You are sure as smooth talker, Mr. Zimmer."

"Arnold."

"Arnold."

"Do you want to stay a while watch the lights?." "Would love to."

"By the way, Mr. Zimmer, thanks," she said, leaned over, and kissed him.

It felt good, amazingly good. There was that little spark again.

"That there, Mr. Zimmer, was special too, my first kiss."

He smiled. "Now that's a treasure," he said. "It was mine too." They laughed.

They sat there, didn't talk, and then they heard the music float up from the ballroom. "Let's go see."

"Why not stay and dance here?" he said.

"I am terrible and would look a fool. I can't dance."

"Then what a perfect place to teach you," he said.

The roof was their dance floor, the city lights the audience, and the pigeons gave approval.

It was perfect.

"Have you seen Hettie?" Danny asked.

"No," Gloria answered. "Last I saw she was going into the foyer."

Danny walked in and inquired if anybody has seen her.

The lift bellhop spoke again. "She's up on the roof with that skinny man with the glasses."

"What boy?" Danny said cross. "Don't know, it's that tall skinny man with the big black glasses."

Danny was going to storm up there. But a soft hand held him back.

"You go up there, Danny Venter, so help me God. I will take my rifle and shoot you."

He turned and looked at Christina.

"She will be fine. Hey, the guy was such a gentleman to buy her that pendant and all."

Danny faltered then Christina said, "Strange that a man that lured me up a church tower to show me the town now suddenly is so concerned. Come show me if you can still waltz. Redeem yourself for all the crap you've made."

Danny looked back at the lift then at Christina.

"I think the waltz sounds just wonderful."

Then he stopped and said to the bellhop, "They leave you find me. You tell me okay?"

It was Byte and his wife that stole the evening when it came to dancing. They were professional, elegant, surefooted, and extremely good.

Samantha tried to do the Charleston, but it looked like a marionette that the strings got tangled up.

Christina stood at one of the windows that overlooked the street.

There was a man walking on the opposite side. He looked up then spat and walked off. Christina let out a small shriek.

"Anything wrong, ma'am?" one of the waiters said. "No, no, I just thought I saw someone I knew."

That man sure looked like Winslow. Jesus I'm losing it. Could have sworn it was him.

As he spat on the ground, Breton Winslow swore, "Fucking rich people hate you, you bastards." With that, he disappeared around the corner.

CHAPTER 5

Sobuza left Danny and made his way east toward where the sun was rising.

The journey would take him nearly a month hiding from the British. Crossing the main road between Durban and Johannesburg was easier than the road down to the Cape. Hills and trees gave lots of cover.

He had been traveling close on three months now and had no idea where he was.

The horse was let go as it was difficult to hide.

Destruction and signs of the war were everywhere to be seen. Seeing those hurt and maimed was terrible. Most of all talking to fellow black people and hearing about the atrocities that they experienced. How men were brutally beaten and killed, women raped, and children orphaned and left to die. Herded into camps like cattle. Every day he asked himself who where these people, did they not have blood flowing in their veins. His hate for them grew every day.

As he entered a clearing, a large man with a shield and spear stood there looking at some cattle.

He saw Danny raised his spear and ran over Danny stood still. The man stopped. The thorn trees, long grass, and anthills was Africa at its most beautiful. Two black men, one in full war attire, the other in thread bare pants and torn shirt with a rifle.

"What you want?" the man said in Zulu.

Sobuza understood Zulu and could even speak some. The Swazi and Zulus don't sit; at the same fire ages of war and strife had made them enemies. Sometimes they were friends then enemies again.

Sobuza sat down on the ground.

"This stupid baboon of a man had lost his way. He had strolled into the house of the mighty, Zulu. If the mighty warrior would be so kind as to just point in the direction, he would be gone running away like jackrabbit back to the dung heap where all Swazi baboons belong."

The Zulu smiled.

"I can see you're a man that knows his place in live.

I can help people like you, people who know who is the mightiest of all warriors."

The man raised the spear then threw it. "In that direction of my spear travel three days if you're a Zulu warrior, someone that's a mere baboon maybe five days. You'd see the river that skirts the border between the Zulu Kingdom and were the baboons live."

Sobuza backed off then stood up and ran, not with much effort more as show. He could have shot the man, but what would that have proven?

He covered the distance in less than three days.

As he sat on the banks of the Pongola River, the thorn trees and Majestic Mountain in front of him, the smell that came in on the breeze was the smell of home.

Within this mountain range was his home—the place he belonged.

He crossed the river at a low spot, washed himself, then drank some water and started the final leg of his journey thru the hills that was his homeland.

As a young man, he had traveled all over the kingdom wandering, looking, and getting to know this place that was his home. His father had once brought him to a spot not far from here and said as far as the eye can see, it's Cetshwayos land. Never go there, you will not be spared, they will kill you.

The stream he came to flowed from the hills opposite, then came to a small flat section before making its way east to join other rivers going to the sea.

As he looked, he saw the grass, the hills, even a Jakarada tree in full bloom. Swazi land was a landscape taken by God crumbled and then laid flat and smoothed out. Hills and valleys with the occasional high mountain like outcrop. Grasslands with tufts of trees and sprinkled with big granite boulders. Small clear streams flowed to join the bigger orange-colored rivers that made their way to the Indian Ocean. Red hot poker flowers were complimented by lilies and blue and yellow flowers. Big thorn trees—their distinct triangular shape, narrow at the bottom, the branches, mostly without leaves as the game had eaten the new sprouts—shot up some as high as thirty feet where a flattop was the place for small fern like leaves to form a canopy. The trees had big white thorns that would pierce the skin and then with a small barb hold on to the pierced skin. Blue monkeys and weaver birds were all about a thick patch of reeds skirted the bank. On the opposite side was a sandy shore with an odd black rock.

It smelt so good he could smell the fire of the village just across the outcrop with its big granite rocks. To the left, a small path led up toward those rocks. The wind blew slightly making the long grass dance and wave.

As the stream below flowed over a big flat rocky surface, its water clear and dark made a gurgling sound. Small green thorn trees were growing on the opposite bank, with just enough space between them for an animal or human to pass. Barren rocks gray in color lay like giant marbles strewn between them.

Two Hadidas flew over followed by an egret. Someone was coming; he could wait and see who it was. But he decided to first see what and who was coming this way. He entered the long green Reeds taking care so he would not break any and show his presence. He sat down, invisible, unless one really stood and watched to see him.

She came down the path. She was singing, her cloth dress draped over one shoulder, on her head a big silver square-shaped tin. In one hand she had a small basket. There were tassels and beads hanging from her skirt. Her breasts were bear and firm that marked her as a woman that had been thru the rituals and was ready for marriage.

As she sat down on the single boulder as her stool, she started talking to the animals.

"Hey, Mrs. Weaver, that's the second nest he's built for you. What's wrong with you? That nest looks fine to me, you better move in, else he's going to find another female, one that likes his handy work."

She turned to the monkeys. "Why are you lot laughing like that? Shouldn't you be out foraging for food? No, you sit here in the tree with your little bums baking in the sun."

Sobuza smiled but sat motionless.

"Okay," she said, "I did bring you guys some stuff. Come, come, come down. I will give you something."

The monkeys nearly fell out the tree and came within a few feet of her.

"Look at you, bright eyes, you're filthy. Where have you been, better get yourself washed. No guy is going to look at you if you're so dirty."

Holding out a nice big maroela fruit, she said, "Come, come, get it. No ways am I throwing food on the ground." The biggest monkey came to her cautiously, took the fruit gently without grabbing then scooted of.

She fed them all one at a time—different fruits to different animals.

"Okay you lot, of you go. I came here to get some water and bath."

Sobuza took a deep breath.

She heard something, stood up, and looked around looking straight at him. She never saw him. Then slowly, once she was happy, it was safe. She removed her clothes, went into the river, and bathed.

Sobuza was sweating; he was so aroused that if he moved, he would ejaculate.

She washed for about three minutes then dressed, filled the can, and then waving to the, animals she walked off. He waited five minutes then walked into the river, and lay there he had never ever felt that way ever.

It took him fifteen minutes to get to his senses. With his body dripping wet, he walked to where she had been sitting. As he approached, he saw a small armband she had left on one of the stones. He took it and placed it on his lips, then he smelt it and smiled.

Walking up a narrow little path that swung back and forth, he eventually crested the gap in the boulders on the mountaintop. Below him was his village, his house, his people. He sat down and looked. She was nowhere to be seen.

He entered the village with its round dome like huts made of long tree sprouts that had been stripped of their leaves and smaller limbs—they had been woven with others to form crossed lattices. Grass and fine sprouts lashed onto them to form a mat. The dome had no windows blackened by the sun to give it a gray color. Only a small round entrance and in some a hole in the roof in the middle to let the smoke out, from a fire burning inside, was visible.

Years of walking in and around the huts had made the ground hard and bare. There were logs and even some chairs where people would sit outside to talk or watch over there external cooking fires.

He was where his people lived. The queen, the mother, the power of the nation, the first wife, had a hut that was large and could be seen from a distance with a big tree branched fence around it.

He walked in that direction and was stopped by two men bearing spears. They had the traditional clothes of men. This made Sobuza feel uncomfortable wearing a shirt and cut of pants. The soft tanned impala hide that covered their loins shimmered in the sun; on their calves were big white fur of brushed-up goatskin bands, and on their upper arms feathers, each had a spear in one hand and a knob *kierie* (a stick with a big wood ball on one end) in the other. "Who are you?" they asked.

"It is I, Sobuza, the second son to the queen."

"The queen has no second son. He died more than a year ago."

"No, no, it's me. I am her son."

They didn't move an inch and stood there blocking his way.

Then Sobuza spoke again.

"Mama Nokise Dlamini Will not be too happy to know that some men stopped her son, Sobuza, the son of Sikhanyiso, to come to her. But if you don't want me to go thru, go tell Nokise that Sobuza has gone back because his own people didn't make him welcome."

There was a short discussion then they said he had to come with them.

They took the rifle and with some more men joining them, led him the three—fourth mile to the entrance of the big dome hut of the queen. As he passed, he looked at the people. It was obvious that the war had not affected them drastically. Things were still as they have always been.

The smell of maize burning in pots came to him. An occasional chicken foraging for food or stray goat or dog wandering into their path was chased away by the men with him. People sat, watched, and pointed.

He never saw her even though he looked for her.

Two of the queen's guards stopped them at the gate to the main enclosure. A short discussion ensued, then they took him with them up to the hut.

The main hut was enormous in size, the entrance big, like a normal door. Once at the door, they stopped.

"Who is that man with you? He looks familiar," a voice from within called.

"It is Sobuza, Mother, I have returned." There was a short silence then a shriek and an old lady came running out. "Sobuza."

"Yes, Mother." She ran and grabbed him in her arms.

"You're alive. They told me the soldiers killed you. Look at you, a beard, this clothes. No wonder I did not recognize you."

"Not me, Mother. I am a Swazi. We don't die that easy." He laughed.

A big man came out of the hut.

He was dressed the same as the other men, but he had red feathers around his neck and wore a leopard skin cloth instead of an impala skin. The sign of royalty.

"So the man they sent to go find me has returned. He didn't do a good job. It seems I had to make my own way back, you're just as useless as you've always been."

With that, he walked right past Sobuza without as much as a how are you.

Sobuza was hurt. All the trouble, hurt, and danger he had been thru was because of his elder brother. Now he can't even say thanks for coming for me, glad to see you're safe. The mother saw and said, "He changed. He's not the good person he was. The city has poisoned his soul.

Sobuza knew better.

A big feast was held, but the elder brother, Lusuke, didn't attend.

At this feast, he saw her. She was one of those bringing food and beer to the people sitting and enjoying themselves while some of the men and woman danced by the light of a big fire. The sparks and crackle of the fire would send big plumes of sparks in the air that would dance about like fireflies before they died.

She came to him and asked if he wanted a beer.

"Your name?" he asked Yensiwe. She said, "Beer would be good." He held out a hollowed-out calbas that she filled with home brew beer.

She was about to leave when he gently took her arm.

She stood there perplexed. Then he slowly tied her bracelet on her arm. She looked and realized he had seen her when she was bathing. She put her hand to her mouth and then was about to run off blushing when he said, "Yensiwe, I closed my eyes. Never looked," he lied. She smiled then said, "Thanks," but she knew that he was lying. It made her feel less embarrassed. Maybe he didn't look.

Sobuza made a point of seeing her each day then just talking everyday talk. About what had happen while he was gone and what was she doing. It didn't take long for both to realize that things were getting mighty serious. Sobuza had very little even if he was second in line to the throne; he would still be required to give a lebola, a dowry for this girl. He had to make plans to get that. How he wasn't certain.

It is life, destiny, that for some people, just when they think they are looking down at the world from a cloud, and they are feeling so happy and so good that life sweeps them off their feet for them to fall down in the dirt and grime. They had struggled so long to get out of.

It was obvious something was going on. Everywhere people were talking and women were shouting. Some young girls ran about like mad people shrieking.

Lusuke had announced that by sunset tomorrow, he will choose a wife. Pressure from the elders had forced his hand. Lusuke spent his days looking at cattle, training his men to fight, and be hard. Marksmanship with spears and with knob *kieries* where what fueled him.

They had told him that his mom was not getting younger, neither was he. The clan required that the lineage was guaranteed, he needed to take a wife, bear sons, so that everybody would be happy.

Mothers groomed and tended to their daughters rubbing their skin with maroela oils to make them shine and make their breast look more pointed. The hides were cleaned and cleaned and cleaned again, each bead washed.

Every girl that was eligible to be married was there and had to be there. Sobuza cringed. Yensiwe was standing amongst them. She was required to; no young available woman was excluded.

Lusuke came into the gathering flanked by a group of warriors he trained with every day. He smiled as he saw all the woman.

Then in a loud voice, so all could hear, he said, "The leopard will today take a woman, a woman that can bear him sons, lots of sons that will grow up and be as strong as their father. A man that knows no fear." He beat his chest. Everybody shouted applause and then in Swazi, "The king to be."

Slowly he walked amongst the woman, smiled at this one touched an arm on that one walked around another. He had been doing this for half an hour and then came to Yensiwe.

He looked at her. She just looked straight ahead. Lusuke walked around her, looking at her as if she was one of his cattle.

Then he looked up straight at Sobuza, smiled, and said, "I have made my choice." Sobuza knew he knew how he felt about Yesiwe. He knew he had done this deliberately. There was nothing he could do. Lusuke was the king to be and could do as he wanted.

Taking Yesiwe by the arm, he announced, "Yesiwe will be my wife." Sobuza saw her look at him, saw his pain as he saw hers. He turned and walked away slowly, but this was not to be. Lusuke called on him. "Don't you agree with my choice, brother? You're leaving?" Sobuza stopped then turned around with a big forced smile. "The king to be had surely chosen the best." Lusuke wasn't sure what to make of this. His first fear was that Sobuza had been with her and that she was not a virgin anymore. "We will see," he said, this time with some doubt. "The elder woman will tell me that." "I'm sure they will," Sobuza smiled again. Then walked off. Luskuke was confused by the answer and the way in which Sobuza had just left off. By tradition Yesiwe had to go with the elder woman. An inspection would be carried out, and if she was not a virgin, she could be killed. As special as she was chosen by the king, she would not be spared. It would also be the same for the man that had been with her without the traditional form of marriage.

Sobuza walked for the whole night then sat on top of a big rock overlooking the countryside. He shouted, "You elders, why you do this to me? I have done you no harm. You get me beaten, pissed on, let me wander thru a land where people were trying to kill me. Now you make me fall in love with Yesiwe then you give her to Lusuke. Why, why, why, why?"

He sat there on that rock for two solid days.

People came from the outlying villages to attend the royal wedding. Sobuza did not want to be there. He left the village, did not want to see or be near the event.

Life carried on even though it was extremely painful for Sobuza. Lusuke would make sure that Sobuza would be called to his royal hut. Then he would have Yesiwe serve them and tell Sobuza what a wonderful wife she was, how she pleased him, and that soon she would bear his sons. He told Sobuza that he made sure of that by having sex with her sometimes three times a night and even in the day.

Sobuza realized that the only way to stop this was to play his game. He would ask Lusuke intimate questions about their sex life and lick his lips as though he would get some evil pleasure if Lusuke told him. Lusuke never did. He actually stopped talking about her because it did not seem to affect Sobuza in any way. Inside Sobuza died over and over again. Lusuke could just as well have taken a knife and skinned him alive. But he bore the pain and did what the king to be required.

Lusuke might have been a great warrior, a man with an evil streak, a bully and a mean person. One thing he wasn't, he wasn't fertile.

After three months, Yesiwe still didn't show any sign of being pregnant. Lusuke ridiculed her, even beat her for not bearing him children. He took a second wife with the same result then took three, more, all at the same time, and none of them bore him children. Sobuza was ecstatic. The mighty warrior was not a man after all.

Witch doctors, the elders, everybody tried to help but to no avail. It didn't occur to Lusuke that while being in Johannesburg and he had, had a good time with everybody, he drank some of the local home brew that contained mercury that combined by an over exercising program had not just lowered his testosterone but made him completely in fertile.

To say the elders were upset and were worried made things worse for Lusuke. He felt that other men were pointing at him and that someone had placed a spell on him.

He decided that it would be Sobuza. He brought him to his enclosure, had him beaten, and then demanded he own up to the spell. Sobuza would rather die than lie, he said nothing. The men were laying into Sobuza with their sticks when a big hush fell over the enclosure.

Nokise stood in the gate. Lusuke stood up. She pointed at him and said, "Down like the rest."

He was going to argue, but the look on her face said everything. She walked over to the barely conscious body of Sobuza. Then she turned and said, "If my son dies, no one. Let it be known no one will leave this enclosure alive."

Then she turned to Lusuke. "That includes you. You behaved like a spoiled kid. You dishonor our family and the clan by treating your brother this way like a common street dog. I will be back at dawn. No one leaves. My guards will stay at the gate. If I return in the morning and he is not on his feet to greet me, or if he is not at least standing, I will kill five men. That will happen each hour during the day. This will happen till he talks and stand on his own two feet."

Then she turned and walked out of the enclosure.

There was at least five minutes of dead silence; then, Lusuke screamed with a voice that sounded like a wounded animal.

"Get him up. Get water, get him attended to or we all die."

A whirlwind hit the enclosure, so it seemed everybody was running around. Water blankets every medicine they could get they got.

"I need you to help me." Yesiwe stood there inside his hut. "Yes."

"If Sobuza doesn't get better and very quickly, we will all die."

"To be honest, o big leopard," she said, "it would be an honor to die with you."

He was going to hit her, but he couldn't afford it. She was his only hope. He had known all along there was something between her and Sobuza way back, and he hated it. That is why he took her as his wife. He wanted Sobuza to hurt.

"He will respond to your touch if you tend to him. Please I need your help."

"Your humble servant can't do that, dear leopard. I am your wife. I cannot go or be near another man. You know the tribal law."

"I don't care about tribal law. I need him on his feet by morning, or my men and eventually me and you, we will die. Nokise will kill us. I saw that in her eyes. I instruct you to go to his hut even if you don't touch him, just talk to him. Please, I beg, the leopard begs." Yesiwe loved it. This pig, this mean man, was begging her after the way he treated her like she was a piece of meat, an object for, his, pleasure. How he hurt her, beat her. She wasn't going to give in so easy. "My husband, don't ask your wife to do this, please. It's not right. I have been a loyal wife," she said.

"I know, I know, but I ask my wife, my special wife, my first wife to help me."

The other woman saw her enter and then caught their breaths. Sobuza was barely breathing. He had been beaten badly. Big welts were all over his body, and one eye was completely swollen shut. He lay there just about naked with the smallest piece of cloth covering the bottom part of his body.

"Everybody out." They looked at her with surprise. "The leopard had spoken."

"Leave," she said. They scampered out the hut. She came out the door and turned to the guard.

"If anybody, even the big leopard, wants to come in, you stop him. No one, no one comes in." The guard actually stepped back when he saw the look in her eyes. "Yes, Yesiwe, first wife," he said bowing to her.

Tears ran down her cheeks as he soothed his wounds with cold water and home salves. Her touch was gentle but still filled with the amazing love she still felt for him.

Then she sang the same song she sang that first day he had seen her at the stream.

He moaned softly when she sang. She stayed the whole night soothing him, making cold compresses for his head.

Nokise entered the enclosure.

"Where is my second son, Sobuza? Why is he not standing there to greet me?" she asked a whimpering and jabbering Lusuke.

She called her guards. "Take five men. Bring them here, then when I tell you to kill them with your spears you do. Did I not make it clear that if my son Sobuza was not standing here to greet me on his own two feet, that five men would die, and five men after that every hour till he does. Was that not clear?" She turned to Lusuke.

She turned to the shivering pleading men that were on their knees about five yards from her.

She raised her hand to give the command.

A low voice said, "No, Mother, no."

She turned the first rays of the sun shone on Sobuza as he stood outside the entrance of the hut. "No, enough, Mother, enough."

She walked over to Sobuza. "I can see you're still hurting and you have a lot of pain, but I can also see that you have the heart of your father. He was once mauled by a lion, but he was up the next day even though everybody told him he should rest."

Yesiwe came out the hut, bowed to Nokise, and then still facing her backed off. No one else came out. Nokise looked at her then at Sobuza, then at her. "Lusuke sent his wife to tend to you. Does he not know that that is wrong? This is the woman that brought you back from the dead. Lusuke's first wife?"

"She is a good doctor, Mother, a very good doctor. Think she must have some good magic," he said and forced a smile. Nokise turned to Yesiwe then said, "You would bring yourself dishonor to save my son. And because of you, everybody gets to live. You are a remarkable woman. Want you to come over to the main enclosure at noon. Want to talk to you. We can have something to eat."

"Sobuza."

"Yes, Mother."

"Go, lie down before you fall down," she whispered in his ear.

"Yes, Mother."

Walking out, she turned to Lusuke, did not say a word, just looked at him for a good three minutes—three minutes that he died and cringed and blabbered and begged. She never spoke then left.

Sobuza had woken. It was dark in the hut, but he knew he was dreaming a good wonderful dream, and he didn't want to wake up. Yesiwe was signing to him. Her soft hands were touching his swollen cheek and rubbing his arms. Then it hurt like hell as she put some more salve on the wound in his side.

"Sorry," she said. "Did I hurt you?"

"What you're doing here? Lusuke will kill us both."

"No, he will not." She smiled. "He told me to come help you. He instructed me to come help you. Actually he begged me to come help you. He said he knows you'll respond to my touch. Seems he was right." Sobuza looked at her long and hard then said, "Never told you, and I must before I die, I love you."

Then he fell back. She grabbed him and shook him. "Ouch," he said, "why you do that? Why do you scare me like that?"

"Just wanted to see if you still cared."

There was a long silence then she whispered.

"I will, and I always will." He heard his mother's voice and how she was telling everybody what she demanded. "Help me to the entrance. Don't want innocent people dying because of me."

"You sure you can do this?"

"No, but I have to."

After Nokise had left the enclosure, it emptied in an instant leaving Lusuke al alone. Feeling vulnerable himself, he left as well. Tried to get away from the main enclosure as quick as he could. He felt that out in the open, he could run or defend himself against Nokise and her guards at her side. Here he could do nothing.

Yesiwe came out to a totally empty enclosure even the other wife's had scampered out and had gone to their mom's and dad's huts.

She went back in the hut that Sobuza was lying in. He was out cold again. He had fallen down on the big bundle of soft cowhides stone-cold. The cloth covering his manhood had fallen open. She stared at his nakedness, how she had longed for him to be inside her, and with a shock realized she still felt that way. It was not lust, it was love. It was that feeling of being one with the man you love that's she longed for. Feeling guilty, she covered him, threw another hide over him, made sure he had water and that he was comfortable, and then she sat there singing to him.

As the sun rose to noon, she entered the royal enclosure of Nokise. She bowed, exchanged, the royal welcomes.

"Come, come, come. Sit here. How is he doing?"

"He's out cold. But he's okay."

"He's as strong as a lion," she said.

"So what is the secret *muti*? What did you use on him?"

Yesiwe lower her eyes so as not to show how embarrassed she felt.

Did you ever know the big elephant?

"No, I had not," Yesiwe said.

"Well, he was the big lion's best friend."

"Yes, I knew that."

"But what you don't know is that I loved him as much as I loved the lion but could never be with him because I was the first wife and wife of the lion."

Yesiwe was astonished.

"Yes, yes, you may be shocked. But I know it's the same for you with Sobuza. I know because I can see it. He got well not because of the *muti* but because of the love you put in the water and the salves."

"Queen mother, I am the leopard's wife."

"So you are, my dear. But he chose you, to spite Sobuza. He didn't choose you because he cared, loved, or really wanted to be with you. I know that."

Yesiwe said nothing.

She was the queen, the monarch, and had just proven why. She knew everything.

"What I want is that you go back there and make sure my second son gets well. Don't cross the line. Promise, remember you're still the leopard's wife. But that doesn't stop you from giving what you can without being one with him, okay? As for the leopard, I will have one of my guards in the enclosure at all time. If he as much as hears a squeak from you because he hurt you, the guard has been giving instruction to stab him."

"Dear mother, he is my husband."

"That true, and he will act and behave like a husband, not like a cattle buyer."

Lusuke was frantic. He had no children, his mother was waiting to kill him. He had to ask his wife to be kind to his brother, which was inviting trouble. What was he going to do?

It came to him, he would redeem himself by regaining lost territories for his mother. He would fight the Pedi's and the Zulu's and whoever he can and not just show his loyalty but at last prove himself as an excellent warrior.

He found his band of warriors, and they set off without decree, without royal instruction. They just went off to fight a war that no one wanted, to start or fight.

In his frenzy to kill, everything that he met so as to show his bravery as a warrior, he attacked a British patrol guarding the border between the union and Mozambique. It was a massacre, and on the banks of the Komati river, Lusuke and two-thirds of his warriors died in a hail of bullets without as much as wounding any soldier.

The men came into the enclosure. Yesiwe was crying. They carried a litter with a body wrapped in cowhides. They had run for three days and nights to bring his body to his mother.

He was mean. He was an idiot and boastful, but he was her son. She cried, deep tears of sorrow joined by Yesiwe.

"I would have thought you'd be happy," Nokise said.

"He was my husband," Yesiwe cried. "He was my husband."

Nokise realized what an absolute wonderful woman this was.

Her health deteriorated quickly, and within two months, the end was drawing near.

"Sobuza."

"Yes, Mother."

"Call the elders for me."

They crammed into big hut. It was dark, smelt of burnt wood and smoke. Everybody sat on the ground. No one said anything.

She spoke softly barely audible.

"My trusted advisers and friends. My time has come, and I know I will not see another full moon. In all the time as your queen, I listened to your advice. May I in these my last moments give you some advice? My son here Sobuza will make a good king, and you as elders have the power to appoint him if you want to. Seeing my son Lusuke is dead. That would make a dying woman very happy, but what would make me live happily in the afterlife with those that had gone, the big lion and the elephant, is if the elders saw it fit to give all the wives of my Lusuke to Sobuza after their mourning. They have no children, let them be honored thru him. Let him take the linage further thru the wife's of Lusuke. So they will not be childless and shamed."

People wept and cried; her body was taken to one of the hilltops then they placed her there wrapped in the skin of a lion. And everybody in the clan from far and wide, placed rocks on her to entomb her forever. The pyramid of rocks could be seen for miles. Even though it was two miles from the main village, it was clearly visible on its hill.

As she had requested, it was done.

Sobuza was inaugurated as the new king. He would be known as the bull elephant, the wise one, in a big ceremony. All five wives of Lusuke was given to Sobuza. He was happy, but having Yesiwe as his wife after years made

Sobuza the happiest man on earth. He went with each wife one each night and the last was Yesiwe. She was cross with him. "You make me wait till last while you lay with them." She hit him on the head with a calabash.

He just stood there, did not say a thing.

"Aren't you going to say anything to me?" She stood there, hands on her hips. The flame inside the hut played on her face and body.

"I died the day he took you. I was going to feed myself to the crocodiles. I watched day in and day out how he used you, how he abused you, make fun of you, smeared your name, made you like some common free woman. But thru it all, I never ever stopped loving you. He could have your body, I had your heart. That is what counted. His other wives, that was duty I did, what was required by my late mother and the elders.

"But you, my love. I kept you for last so that I knew I didn't have to be with them once I was with you. I can be with you tonight, tomorrow night, and the night after. Yes, it is required that I be with them again sometime till they bear children. But you, Yesiwe, it's not about that. I would be with you, just to sit and talk with you, even if I couldn't be with you as one, and it would give me more satisfaction and pleasure than the other wives could ever give me. Your voice, your smile, your touch is so much more exciting than they can ever be. I kept the best for last because it would not be fair to those poor women, to have to realize that once I was with you, they would not be able to give me what you do. They would never, never, ever get close to the love you give me.

Yesiwe stood. Her tears were freely flowing from her cheeks. She came to him slowly, place her arms round his neck, and buried her face in his chest.

It was obvious to all that Lusuke had been the problem as all five wives, including Yesiwe, were pregnant within a month.

The elders were happy and said it was Nokise smiling on the clan. There was going to be a child to fill the throne once Sobuza died.

As the months past the time came.

In a short stretch of three weeks, five babies were born. Yesiwe was the second to last to give birth to a boy, a fat little baby with round cheeks and a potbelly.

The first three wives all had boys, the last one had a girl, and Sobuza was elated. He wanted a daughter as well.

The wives all loved Sobuza. He was a good and honorable husband. He had done right by them, so they came to him and said, "Our good husband, we as wives, we all have wonderful children. We walk proud because we are mothers and woman now because of you. We know you care and love us all. But long before there was any of us, long before there was Lusuke, there was Yesiwe and Sobuza

"We have talked, and we have decided that Yesiwe must have the title as the first wife. You have never spoken of a first wife and treated us all as equal. But we come as your wives today, and with Yesiwe here with us, we ask do us the honor you have given us. Make Yesiwe your first wife."

Sobuza sat for a long while then he spoke. "The queen Nokise looks on us today and she's proud. You have done her and the clan proud. You walk tall amongst the people of our clan because you are royalty, only wives that are really queens, have the ability and knowledge to do what you've just done. As she is proud, I am proud to have each and every one of you as my wife. Proud because of what you ask. My answer would be this—only if she accepts it will I give it."

A long silence again as everybody in the hut looked at Yesiwe. She said nothing just nodded her head in a yes motion.

The impromptu feast lasted for two days.

As he walked thru the village with his four sons and daughter, it was this small band that followed him. They were all the same age by a few days if a week. Everybody loved it. They waved and shouted. The clan was good. It was happy; the evil days of Lusuke were gone.

Sobuza would spend hours teaching the small band of sons what it was to be a man, to be strong, to be tough, to be proud, to be a warrior for the nation.

By eight years old, the band was the terror of the village when they were seen people would be ready. Trouble in some sort of mischief was to follow. There leader was Poko, Yesiwe's son. He's little potbelly had gone away and was replaced by muscle of a small boy. The love Sobuza had for all his sons were unsurpassed. But Poko was his favorite, and everybody knew that. Sobuza would educate him in things that the other sons would never know. He taught him the ways of being a chief, had him sit in on clan meetings. As a small boy, Sobuza loved how he looked with his fat little belly, standing with his spear, looking out on the courtyard at nothing just like Sobuza himself would do.

This was their son, their son made by them thru love. His and Yesiwe's.

Father David Dowes was the catholic priest that had won favor with Sobuza and was allowed to build a small church on the outskirts of the village. A good man, a quick look, would take him to be a friar or Jesuit, big long brown frock with the rosary beads hanging around his neck. Stocky man with a big bald patch on his head rimmed with short-cut gray hair, a voice thick like a base drum. He walked slowly with a swagger like a sailor.

Sobuza and David would sit for hours. David would teach Sobuza English, and Sobuza would teach him Swazi. Needles to say, the band of sons and the daughter on insistence by all the wives would be there and would be taught at the same time at least three times a week. Yesiwe would often tell Poko not to talk to her in English. When he spoke to her, he would speak Swazi.

The sun shone on the meadow, were Sobuza's cattle where feeding. The four boys were delegated and given the task of watching them, herding them from pasture to pasture.

They saw the two men coming, riding up with their horses. Looking ragged and worn, one had an old soldier's helmet, and the other had a bowler hat.

As they rode up to the boys, Poko stepped forward. "Stop," he said, "you can't go further." He spoke Swazi.

"Now listen here, little black idiot, we are here to take these cattle to our ranch. We want them, and we want to sell them."

"No, you cannot take my father's cattle," Poko replied in English.

"Look at that, he speaks English. Can you believe it? Can't care who or what your father is. I am taking them. Get out of my way."

He was going to ride to herd the cattle, but Poko stepped in front of his horse.

"These cattle is King Sobuza's cattle. No one takes the king's cattle."

"Listen, you little shit, get out my way. Haven't got time to argue with kids."

Poko stood firm. The horse a few inches from him.

"No you go back."

The hose reared up and the man's helmet came off falling on the ground.

"Fucken little shit bugger of."

"No," said Poko. Then he lunged forward and stabbed the man in his leg with his small spear.

The man screamed in pain clutching his leg.

"The little bastard stuck his spear in me."

"Go," Poko said standing there defiant—a small boy holding his ground against a grown man on a horse.

"Enough of this shit."

The rider pulled out his revolver and shot Poko at close range.

The bullet went right thru his small chest spraying blood and then dust as it hit the dirt behind him.

Poko was flung back violently and was dead before he hit the ground.

The other boys ran as fast as they could putting as much distance as they could between the man and his revolver

He fired some shots but never came close to hitting any of them. They stopped about a half-mile away and turned around.

The two men were herding the cattle heading to the path that would take them to Barberton.

When they felt safe, all of the boys ran back to Poko, where he lay dead, still clutching his spear.

Fear grabbed them. They had to take his body back to the village, and they knew Sobuza was going to be broken, angry, and even blame them for not helping Poko. Wrapped in some grass and sticks, they made a litter and carried the boy's lifeless body back to the village.

The screams and shouts reached Sobuza long before they came into the enclosure. As they entered, Sobuza ran to them. "What is going on, what happened?"

No one spoke, too scared to say a word.

Trembling he unwrapped the grass and sticks, to look into the dead face of his beloved Poko.

His pain, agony, and scream was heard thru the whole Village. Yesiwe came rushing out, and she knew long before she saw the body what had happened.

She sat there with the body of his son in Sobuza's arms. He looked like a rag doll, collapsed. His body was shaking, not saying anything, no sound. Yesiwe sat next to him.

He had been there for hours when one of the elders came to ask if he could help.

They backed off terrified when they saw the look in Sobuza's eyes. It wasn't hate, it wasn't pain. It was more than that. It was a demon looking back at the elders.

After two days, he stood up. The body had started to decompose, but Sobuza didn't seem to notice.

With his son in his arms, he walked to the hill where Nokise was buried and lay him down. Within seconds, the elders were there wrapping the body in hides then backing off.

He found a rock and placed it on the wrapped corpse.

They came from every corner of the kingdom small and old. Some were carried there placing stones on the body that eventually was raised to a small mound, lager than that of Nokise. Sobuza just sat there. No words, no water, no food. Seven days. He sat there in one spot. He got up and walked back to the enclosure.

The other sons didn't want to come close to him out of fear for retribution.

"You've been summoned by Sobuza." They just about crawled into the enclosure.

Sobuza sat the in the middle and waved them over.

Four small boys were just about wetting themselves with fear. "Come," he said, "come." They scrambled over and sat at his feet close but not too close so they could make a run for it if they saw their life's in danger.

"What happened?" is all he said.

There was silence.

Again he said, "What happened?" This time with more urgency.

They were scared this was the question they feared, and now they had to answer.

They related the events to him in every detail.

Sobuza smiled. "My Poko defended my cattle with his life, stood his ground against a man with a gun." Tears ran down his face. "Even in his death, he makes me proud."

"You boys did well. You came back for him. I am proud of you too. You did not just run away and leave him so some jackal could eat him."

Then they all burst out in tears. The relief of not being in deathly trouble was overwhelming, and they came over so he could hold them.

"The hat the man was wearing, what did it looked like?" he asked.

Jabbering, each gave what he thought to be the description. The smallest in stature, Kabi, said, "The hat should still be there. It fell off when the horse reared up."

"I will go fetch it."

"No," Sobuza said, but it was too late. Four boys were out, and on their way to get the hat they knew was important.

Sobuza bellowed to his guard, "Follow them. Make sure they are not hurt. Guard them with your life."

He looked at the helmet and he knew it well: the Royal British badge with lion, with a crown and unicorn holding a shield above the shield with all its markings another lion with a crown. Underneath was written in Latin: "My God and my right shall I defend."

Sobuza had seen it many times during the war. It was on many banners worn by most soldiers. He had grown to hate that symbol. Now it was his goal to destroy whoever was telling the people to do the evil they have been doing.

In any war, it's the innocent—the everyday citizens—that pay the biggest price. Soldiers follow orders, kings and generals give the orders without being involved or even full understanding what the effects and consequences would be. They do as they are advised to do. They do what they feel is needed to protect and guard, what it is they believe in, be it king, country, or land.

Many misuse those privileges. Many don't even for one second realize that by wearing these symbols they are representatives of that cause.

The man that had shot Poko was a thug and villain, a vagrant, out to get what he could for himself at all cost .Wearing the old British soldiers helmet was an act of protection, not representation. He could not care less, but it had some sentimental value, and he wore it as a symbol of the fact that he had been in the terrible Boer war. Fifteen years had passed; yet that's all he had, was a time when he was respected, honored, and had power. That's what this man had clung to.

The events had changed Sobuza; protection of his other sons was paramount at all time. They had a guard with them. Any excursions or breaking away from the protection would be followed by a good hiding with a *sjambok* (rawhide whip).

Although Yesiwe bore him more children, all were daughters. He loved them, but a part of his soul died the day Poko was killed.

Two weeks after the killing, he and Father David had made the journey to Barberton, logged a complaint, and asked that the man that killed the son of the king be brought to justice.

When he returned a month later, nothing had happen. No one had even tried to find the man. Father David had his hands full to keep Sobuza calm and not to cause a big problem in Babarton.

"Ten heads of cattle for the man that finds the killer of my son. Find him, kill him, if he tries to flee, but if possible, bring him to me alive."

As the word spread, everybody was out looking.

The four men came running up to the gate of the enclosure. They had a torn, a bloodied tunic.

"O honorable king, we had found this evil snake and scorpion of a man. We had chased him. He fled. We never stopped. We chased him for two days even though he had a horse. When he came to the big Komati River, the horse stumbled when it went down the bank and broke a leg. But he ran into the water and tried to swim across to get to the other side. Dear king.

"The crocodiles showed no mercy, dear king. They tore his limbs and head from him like he was a straw doll. We found his clothes down river, close to one of the lairs of the crocs. Here it is."

"You sure it was him?"

"One of the Venda people had seen him with your cattle. We found the cattle as well. He had sold it to a Portuguese trader. We just took them back."

It did help Sobuza in a strange way that this evil man had died the way he did. But it didn't stop him from hating. The person, the king who gave the orders for these men that came over the land like ants killing and destroying everything, had to answer. This king made one of his men kill Poko.

The two men that entered the enclosure wore pith helmets, dressed in khaki clothes, each carrying a case and some maps.

"You are?" Sobuza asked in broken English.

"We are here to ask the king for permission," they said. They were going to explain why and what they were doing but never got that far.

Sobuza exploded with anger and lashed out knocking the one man to the ground breaking his glasses.

"What is this?" Sobuza pointed to the badge on the case the man carried.

Again before the man could answer, Sobuza shouted.

"You come to my enclosure, and you bring this to my house, this evil thing. You will die today. The men started crying and begged and tried to talk, but Sobuza just pointed and said, "Keep quiet. You are in the presence of the mighty elephant. I am the king, the king from the Dhlamini family, the son of the great Nokise. This thing, this evil you bring with you, who does it belong to? Who is the man that sent you to bring this thing to my land, to my kingdom?" Sobuza said pointing at the crest on the briefcase.

Again Sobuza didn't wait to hear the answer. This was the opportunity he had longed for. He had two men of the king in his grip. He would force the king to come to him, or these men would die a very, very slow and hard death."

He wrote the letter himself.

To the king of this evil on this bag. One full moon and you come to my village. You come to set your men free, or I will slowly and painfully make them pay, it will take days. Come and face me like a man, not the coward that sends his men.

Father David tried to intervene, but Sobuza didn't listen. He just wanted father David to check the letter then made sure the police in Barberton got it.

The man they bought to the enclosure had been beaten badly. He was covered in bruises and stank from all the urine and feces that they hand dragged him thru and forced him to eat.

They had taken him as far as they dared without killing him.

The man was about thirty years old, a beard that was now caked with filth.

He was lying on the ground with one of the warriors standing on his back pressing him into the dirt.

"Bow to the mighty elephant."

Sobuza spoke slowly in English.

So this is the mighty king that sends the warriors across the land to kill women and children, to rape and murder, to shoot innocent children guarding cattle. It is not that wonderful if you get what you have told others to do. It's not so good if you are on the receiving end of things, you bloody snake. He hit him with the fist on the side of his head. Then he kicked him hard against the head. The man just lay there.

Sobuza beckoned his men, and they came over, lifted the man to his knees, and held his head back. Sobuza turned and with his backside inches from the man's face, he farted loudly. The man swallowed back the vomit. Then he spoke, "You fucken black piece of shit. For someone afraid of frogs, you sure look brave. Should have left you in the desert and let the khakis kill you. This is how you treat the man that saved your life, should have shot you myself, you black bastard."

Sobuza froze then turned.

"Daniel? Daniel? No, no, no, no, Daniel."

Danny was in Johannesburg. He had to be to sign some legal documents as he was the only member of the board that was available. The others had gone to Antwerp by ship to attend a meeting with the diamond buyers.

Danny sat in a big office dark wood paneling, was all around green leather covered chairs, were placed in front of a big thick oak desk with a black leather insert, crystal inkwells, and a bolting paper holder made from silver was on the desk. An ornate lamp stood to one side. The shelves behind the desk were covered with rows of books all carefully placed there. Gold and silver banded backings all line up.

On the sidewalls were paintings of table mountain, on the other a painting of a bull elephant in full charge. A big Persian carpet lay on the floor, its deep purple and red patterns and tassels on the end brought warmth to the office. The young man came in out of breath and just about tripped on the carpet when he handed the letter to Daniel.

"We have a problem, sir, a big problem."

"And what is that?" Danny stood up.

"The swazi king Dalmini has taken two of our prospectors captive. He threatens to torture them to death unless the 'king' of this (he pointed to the leather satchel that had come with the letter) comes to free them in person to his Village at Mbabaene. No later than Friday."

"And where is that?" Danny said.

"In Swazi, land east of Baberton."

"Can't anybody else go? You sure there hasn't been some big misunderstanding?"

"We thought of it, but if someone else went, and he found out, he might kill everybody. You'll have to go, sir. We will make sure you have guards and you will be well armed. He said if we don't send the *king*, he will kill whoever comes for our prospectors. We thought of sending someone that could say they were the *king*, but the risk is very high if he found out we tried to fool him."

"Well then, we better get moving. It's Wednesday, and God knows if we will be there by Friday." Send my wife a message telling her I will be out of town and will be back on the farm by Monday."

Getting to Barberton was a long journey, by train, thru Middelburg then Machadodorp, then down the valley at Waterfall Bo and Waterfall Onder, then to Nelspruit from there by car down to the fever valley of death before reaching the town. Here they went by horseback up the Saddle back pass to reach the border between the union of South Africa and Swazi land.

With full cultural dress, the seven warriors waited for Danny to arrive.

Once he had gotten to the border, only he was allowed in. No one else. Danny didn't see any problem and even told his people he would be back early in the morning. Just sort out the misunderstanding," he said.

Three days later, the two prospectors returned and had no news what had happened to Danny.

They were barely out of sight of those waiting at the border when he was attacked violently. They laid into him with Shambucks and sticks. Danny had no defense. They beat him brutally then dragged him thru small thorn trees and thru dug. They proceeded with him to Sobuza's main enclosure. But it never stopped. All the way, they just beat him and humiliated him, urinating on him, defecating on him, rubbing his face in their fesses. Made him eat it. Danny had no idea what was going on, why were they doing this, what had he done wrong to deserve such treatment. No one was here to help no one to hear his calls. He was at their mercy.

As they passed the church, Father David tried to stop them, but they threatened him with death as well.

With one eye badly swollen, a cut lip, an ear that looked like a cauliflower and smelling like the pits of hell, they reached the enclosure and threw him on the ground.

Then one man just went and stood on his back, and the pain to Danny was unbearable.

The chief came out, but Danny could hardly see him. He made a lot of noise, said a lot of things, then came over lifted Danny's head, and slapped him hard. Danny did not see any of it coming and was just about to pass out when his head was lifted again. This time the chief came up, turned around, and farted right in Danny's face. He coughed and chocked, and thru his blood-streamed eyes, he saw it. The shape of a *z*, on the leg of the chief.

It cannot be, Danny thought. Yet it was. He who would know that z shape anywhere.

"You fucken black piece of shit. For someone afraid of frogs, you sure look brave. Should have left you in the desert and let the Khakis kill you. This is how you treat the man that safe your life? Should have shot you myself, you black bastard."

Danny passed out

"Danny? No, no, Danny, no!"

Sobuza cradled Danny's head in his arms.

"Water, quick, quick, water! Then after washing Danny's face, he started hitting his men with a long stick.

"Who did this? Who did this? Who, who?" They scrambled, not knowing what was happing. The king had gone mad.

One of the elders went to Sobuza and grabbed his arm.

"You told them to do this. You said they must do this. They were doing what you wanted them to do."

"No, no, not to this man. No, no, he's not the king. I know this man. He's not the king."

"Get help, quick!" Sobuza was up again. "Get him to my hut quick! Water and medicine quick. We need to help him move. Move quick, quick!"

No one had any idea what was going on.

Someone went and called Father David.

As the witch doctors and Yesiwe were working as hard as they could, everybody tried to make the pain less, dress his wounds get rid of the stinking clothes.

Sobuza ran to the prospectors and was about to put his spear into them.

"Why you, why you tell me that Danny is the king of this?"

"He is, he is! That is the badge for the South African Mineral Diamond Mining Corporation. Danny is one of the board members, one of the chiefs."

"No no no," Sobuza shouted.

"Danny is not the king of this." He held up the helmet with its badge.

It was Father David that came to help.

"That's King George's badge, the king of England and South Africa. "This badge is the mining badge. See?" Father David pointed. "There is a lion, here is a leopard with no crown, here is a unicorn, there is a zebra, and then at the top is a mine worker's helmet, not a crown."

Sobuza looked and looked again. Sure the badge on the satchel was different than the one on the helmet. He sat back, put his head in his hands, and cried aloud.

"Go, go, go home," he said to the men.

They just left, never saw Danny, just got out there as fast as they could in the middle of the night.

Sobuza kept saying he was sorry and kept begging for forgiveness. He had just almost killed the one man that had thru his whole life showed him compassion, saved him from certain death. This man had treated him as an equal, even gave him a gun to defend himself, gave him food, helped him.

"It was a mistake, Danny, it was a big mistake. I am so sorry, my friend, so sorry."

Danny said nothing, just looked at him, with pain and hatred in his eyes.

As he sat there outside the hut still not able to walk, Yesiwe and Sobuza's daughter came and sat next to him. Thru the daughter who could speak English very well due to the efforts of Father David, she started with the whole story of Sobuza and Nokise of the brother, of Poko, how he suffered, how he hurt, how he hated and how that had eaten him alive like ants eat flesh. How he was blinded by his anger and never saw the difference in the badges.

Danny listen but did not say a word.

With the help of a knob kierie as a walking stick, Danny went over to Sobuza.

"Come," he said loud, "you and me we need to talk."

Then he turned around and walked to the dead heap of burnt firewood and sat on a log.

He came slowly and muttering and not sure what to expect and sat next to Danny. They were nearly touching.

The two men talked from early morning till late in the night: no water no food, someone lit the fire and was gone.

Everybody knew that this was important. This was life or death. One of them could easily die right there by the fire.

At times they were shouting at each other, at times both men sobbed like kids.

"You need to stop the hate. We need to stop the hate, Sobuza, we need to." Danny said.

"My wife Christina, she has a lot of hate she carries with her every day. She is looking for revenge. She hopes that it would set her free. Stuff from the concentration camp, it's like a big sore in her soul that doesn't want to heal."

"I hate the English for what they did to us. They wiped out a whole generation of my people. I can go on hating and die a bitter sad man, Sobuza, but I will not. My daughter has met a man. He is a Khaki, as British as it gets. I could stop her from loving him. I could hurt her, do the same hate-thing all over again and watch her resent me and hate me."

"Or I can step back and look at the young man a man with lots of guts, clever, observant." Danny quickly told him about the necklace.

"But most off all, I have no doubt they love each other and that the children, the two of them, will bring into the world will be a new generation that doesn't see Khaki or Boer but sees themselves as South Africans."

"We, me and you, we need to stop this. Look at us, your hate nearly killed me. Why can't we live together?"

It was quiet for a long, long while; then, Sobuza got up and went and stood in front of Danny.

"I know the words I say will not take away what has happened to you. Neither will the memories ever fade. But Danny, my friend, I ask forgiveness. That's all I can ask. As for my people and my house, never ever will we look at a white person in any other way as just a fellow human being. Your company and yours alone will have free access to any part of my kingdom to drill to mine, and I don't want anything in return."

Sobuza was about to say something else when Christina came walking into the enclosure. It was obvious, she was cross, very cross. The guards were shouting, but Sobuza stopped them. She saw Danny and ran over.

"Are you okay?"

"Yes, just beaten up a bit."

"Dammit, Daniel, why did you come here by yourself? Look at you, we thought you had been murdered. No one knew what happened to you."

Christina had got worried when the two prosecutors return and no Danny.

She asked the police for help, but they really didn't want an incident or something that would start any conflict between Swazi land and South Africa. They had sent people to inquire, but everybody was quiet.

"If no one wants to find out where my husband is, I will do so myself."

She called her guard. "Get the car! We are going to Swazi land right now."

When she was stopped at the border, the warriors quickly realized that this woman was not to be messed with or confronted. They also knew that she had something to do with the man that the king had at his enclosure. They feared more trouble from the king if they attacked her as well, so they just waved her thru.

"Sobuza, this is my wife, Christina."

"What happened?" was all Christina said.

Yesiwe came from the hut when she heard the shouting and saw the white woman standing in the enclosure. She heard them talk.

"What is going on?" she asked her daughter.

The daughter translated.

There was a moment of silence. How do you explain to the wife of a man that saved your life once that you had had him beaten and abused?

Sobuza was about to speak, but Danny stopped him.

Everybody listened to what Danny was going to say.

"The king saved my life. I was attacked by a band of thugs. They nearly killed me. He never realized that they were around, else he would have given me more protection. All he wanted was to see me. I saved his life in the war, and he wanted to thank me by giving me the rights to mine in his kingdom personally. So he saved my life, in the aftermath of it all, everybody tried to tend my wounds and looked after me. With Sobuzas men hunting down the band of thugs, no one thought about letting you know. We just talked a few seconds ago that he would send a runner to the police in Barberton to let everybody know I am okay."

"Too late," Christina said. "The person that needed to know now knows." Then she cried hugging him.

Sobuza looked at Yesiwe. She was crying as well. Danny had not just spoken but proved that he would not entertain the hate that consumes the human soul.

Yesiwe walked over took Christina's hand and led her into the hut with her daughter in tow.

The two of them spoke long into the night. Christina was given water to wash, food, and even some traditional clothes. She heard about how some of the Swazi people had come back after the war telling about their ordeals in the black concentration camps. It made Christina cross all over again.

When she came out later, Danny and Sobuza were still at the fire. Danny let out a long whistle. "Hell, Christina, you look so amazing in that?"

Yesiwe laughed and clapped her hands when she saw the smile on Danny's face.

"Danny Venter," she said. "You're hurt. You're in pain, so much so you can't let your wife know where you are. Don't you even think, don't even think of it."

When Christina found out the truth later when he told her, she was cross with him for a week.

Hatred kills the soul and never brings happiness. No, it's justice that triumphs and brings the release to a burdened heart.

CHAPTER 6

Her flaming red hair flew back as she rode the horse at full speed. It gave the illusion that her head was on fire.

Arnold tried to keep up but was way outclassed.

The wheat fields flew past there green in stark contrast to her hair.

She stopped at her tree then dismounted and waited for him to arrive.

The young man had made an amazing impact on the richest men in the world and their wife's. He had saved them in a way that only a young man with a young girl could have.

Arnold had been spared the war because his father had made a doctor declare him unfit due to his bad eye sight.

Nothing they offered him made him budge.

The boardroom had a long broad stink wood table with twenty-two chairs, ten on each side, and one at each end. Thick green velvet curtains hug in front of the windows. The pictures of the board members and the late Bait hung on the walls. A picture of Queen Victoria hung above the head of the table

On the opposite side was the new Crest of the Union of South Africa.

The floors were bear. The sound of the hustle and bustle of Johannesburg filtered in with the sunlight.

"Gentleman," he said.

"It s an honor to be here in your boardroom, to be able to speak to all of you. But I need you to understand, nothing I did was to attain something in return. I am who I am, you offering me promotions over the heads of men that had been working for years in your company is wrong and cruel. I wish to work my way up like everybody else take my medicine, like every other employee. That's the only way I can do it. That way I will know what it is that makes a place like this work. We all know its people. Thanks again, but I absolutely decline any form of promotion or any special post created for me. It's wrong, and it also makes Hettie Mr. Venter's daughter a commodity that is being used by all of us. Sorry can't allow that."

Thanks again if there is nothing else would like to get to my work; when he got to the door, he turned.

"I take it I can book this time as company time, would not like to lose a day's pay."

"Sure sure," they all said, and he was gone.

As Danny left the boardroom, there was a note from Arnold.

Dear Mr. Venter.

Would just like to discuss a small matter with you if possible outside company time. Say at 3:00 pm at the town hall tearoom down the road at Rissik Street.

Normally Danny would not give such a note a second glance, but this time, he made sure that he notified his secretary that he would be out of office at three to go for a walk.

He stood up as Danny came to his table, then once Danny had sat down, he sat down as well.

"What will it be, gentleman?" the Indian waiter asked.

"Coffee for me, black," Danny said.

"Coffee for me too with milk and sugar, one spoon."

"So, young man, what is it that you like to talk to me about?"

"Mr. Venter, I asked you here to inquire if there would be any possibility of me courting you daughter, Hettie."

This was a major step for Danny. Here was a Khaki asking if he could court his daughter?

"Have you asked her?"

"No. Needed to get your permission first."

"I see," said Danny, "and what are your intentions?"

"Well, sir, would like to get to know her better and pursue the idea of a more lasting and deeper relationship developing between us."

Danny sat there and looked at Arnold. This was a Rooineck, yet he saw in this young man a depth and a honesty he never thought could be in an English man.

He could live with hate and resentment, or he could allow this young man into his life and into his daughter's life. This was a major decision. It felt like he was betraying everything he had fought for and saw his friends die for.

"Well said," said Danny. "Now listen to me, Mr. Zimmer."

"You can court my daughter. If I find out you've dishonored her, made her pregnant, or broke her heart, I will personally take out you liver with a blunt spoon and then eat it after I cooked it on an open fire. Are we clear?"

Arnold wasn't sure if he should smile or cringe.

"Absolutely, sir."

"Then you have my blessing," Danny said and knew that he actually meant it.

"One more thing, sir," Arnold said.

"Yes," Danny said sipping his coffee.

"Where do I go to meet her. Have no idea how to find her or anything."

Danny was going to tell him she lives at Klein Bakawaan Stad near Bethlehem, but he just said, "At the ladies dormitory down at the university. She studies law."

"Thanks, sir." Arnold smiled.

The rest of the talk was about the horses at the races and about rifles and guns, Danny's favorite subject.

Hettie loved the idea of having Arnold as a boyfriend. She loved the excitement and convinced herself that she was in love with him.

The truth was that the months of her childhood in a concentration camp facing dead corpses and the threat of dying every day seeing evil and decay around her had hardened her. All she ever wanted was to be a normal everyday girl, but she couldn't. Fear of being hurt of losing someone had left her without emotion; she could pretend but never cry. She could play the role of being something but never truly felt it in her heart.

A shield had been placed there long ago by the likes of Breton Winslow, the war, and the camp.

He courted her while she finished her honor degree and now her bar exams.

Looking into his eyes, she saw the love and kindness he wanted to give her. She saw the deep-centered giving of himself. She felt a tinge of guilt, yet she said, "I do," and so she became Mrs. Arnold Zimmer.

A small wedding on the farm, just friends.

Although Danny tried as hard as he could, Arnold refused any assistance from him. He was going to provide for Hettie as best as he could by his own means without any help and money from one of the richest men in the world.

Danny admired that but thought it foolish. Christina was the anchor that kept him at bay. "Leave the children, Danny. Just like you, he wants to make his own way thru life."

They called him Jonathan, a chubby little boy with jet-black hair and big brown eyes.

Needles to say, he was spoilt rotten by both grandparents. This upset Arnold, but he knew there was little if anything he could do.

Hettie did not enjoy the child. The fear of Jonathan dying like the children in the camps drove her insane. She didn't want to love the child and then face the pain of losing him. She just couldn't do it. The responsibility of being a mother frightened her and made her afraid. It was Arnold that brought the love and affection. Most nights, it was him who would make a new bottle, rub out the winds, and change the diapers. He talked to his son deep into the night, would sleep during lunch hour at work to try and make up time. Yet he never ever complained not one word.

As soon as possible, Hettie was back at Bain and Taylor, the solicitors she was working for. She had worked hard and was hoping to soon do her final bar exams to be a full-fledged attorney.

Hettie hated what she was doing to Arnold and little Jonathan but brushed it aside as that's life. Arnold was the one that worked hard at getting the romance and the passion in their marriage, but even thou he knew he was not succeeding, he kept at it. The response from Hettie's side was more of an obligation and guilt than of love and affection.

Intimacy was a necessity she had to deal with. It was physical, was quick, and was just an act. She never felt the excitement and the love that was required to make it wonderful.

As the years progressed, it became more difficult. She had violent mood swings and would lash out. In return, Arnold would take Jonathan and just go walking or riding or go to the zoo and visit a lake or the grandparents. Christina knew what was going on and knew why she couldn't do anything.

"Hettie, don't do this to yourself. You were not the reason why things went bad., You were not the reason people died, but they did. I know I am struggling with the same issues, and we are both hurting not just ourselves but those we love. You have a wonderful husband and a beautiful son, don't hurt them. I hurt your father over and over because I carry the hate of the war with me wherever I go. My prayer is that one day I would be able to let go before it is too late. Don't lose precious time with those that love you, don't," Christina said.

The talks helped but never resolved the deeper emotional struggles that Hettie dealt with.

I should have given that boy my bread, and he could have lived. I should have gone up to get the tea for Mom then that little girl would not have been burnt. I should have been the brave one, yet that boy lost his finger to feed his family. Why didn't I cry when people died, why, why? Then the hatred of Breton Winslow, she would wish she could see him and plunge a knife in his heart. She was small when it all happened and could hardly remember what he looked like, just remembered the evil in eyes.

Work and more work, that's what Hettie thrived on.

The man and the little boy sat at the Jukskei river fishing. Arnold had show Jonathan how to set up his tackle. Were and how to cast his line. They would sit there and enjoy the outdoors talking and laughing.

Jonathan loved drawing. He would take an everyday pencil and draw. As he looked at the picture the three-year-old boy had drawn, Arnold caught his breath, no stickmen or stick trees. The little boy had drawn a man a body, a river, a tree, and even some fish. All be it very crude, it looked more like a picture drawn by a ten—or eleven-year-old than a three-year-old.

"Wow, this is very, very good. You like drawing."

"Yes," the boy said shyly.

"Well then, Daddy is going find someone that will help you and you can then draw as much as you want.

"Hettie," he said.

"Come, I want to show you something."

"Can't it wait, Arnold? I am really busy. I am in the middle of a serious divorce case, and have to be ready in the morning."

He handed her the drawing.

"Mm . . . who did this?" she said.

"Jonathan," Arnold said proudly.

"Not bad," she said, turned around, and walked off.

Arnold sat there with Jonathan. They never spoke.

Hettie didn't even know that Jonathan was attending art school after his normal day at primary school.

It was Arnold and his son's secret.

That was Hettie she never saw what was important, only what she wanted to be important.

The pictures hanging in Arnold's small office looked more like black-and-white photos than drawings. Only when one came really close could you see the pencil marks.

He loved it when people would ask about the photos who took them.

"Well, why don't you ask me that question again after you've looked at them very, very closely."

"They are drawings. I will be dammed, and they are amazing drawings. That's stunning. Where did you buy them, they are just out of this world?"

"Well, they were drawn by my son, Jonathan."

"You lie."

"Honest."

"He is only 12 years old. Isn't that true?"

"I know."

"Wow, that's just amazing. You sure it's your son? You're not telling me a lie, are you?"

"No, no, it's my son. I sat and watched him draw the pictures."

The girl that walked into the office looked haggard and worn.

The double door that led out on to Rissik street was the entrance to a big high ceiling foyer with wood paneling and a large desk, behind, which a young man in a white shirt and suspenders sat. To his left was an elevator, and to the right a single door led to an adjoining office. On the door to this office was a sign marked *private* in gold letters.

Behind the young man was a list of names on a large wooden panel with their titles and degrees then followed by a floor and office number.

The man with the girl stepped forward.

"I'm Patrick Murray," he said.

"This here is Joyce Greenham."

The clerk looked at both. "What can we do for you, Mr. Murray?"

"Actually it's Chief Inspector Murray," he said.

"Sorry, sir," the young man said. "My apologies, Inspector."

"This lady is in need of legal assistance."

"What seems to be the problem then?" the clerk asked.

"She has been raped and needed someone to defend her."

The clerk was shocked, he felt like he was looking at something evil and dirty, when looking at Joyce. Rather than getting to involved, he went to find some help.

Tamerin McCloud III was the advocate that came to the front desk.

"Tamerin McCloud III," emphasizing the third part as he held out his hand.

"Chief Inspector Patrick Murray."

"You seem to have a problem then, Inspector?" McCloud said in a tone and manner that would make the queen herself sit up straight.

Patrick explained the situation.

"Well, sir, unfortunately, we don't deal with cases like these."

"You don't? I am positively sure you handled an assault case for the Palmers about a week ago."

"We surely did," McCould said. "But that was a favor for Mr. Palmer."

"So this company only does work for people that are of high Standing, and that has money, as favors?"

"Let's go Patrick. It's no use they will not help us. They are all the same, nobody cares. If you don't have money, you're a nothing."

She turned to leave and walked straight into Hettie who had been standing in the doorway listening.

"That's not quite true," Mc Cloud tried to say.

"Mr. Mc Cloud, may I take the ladies case?" Hettie spoke.

"You certainly may. How do you intend to pay, my dear?" He turned to Joyce. He did this to prove a point.

Before she could answer, Hettie spoke, "It would be a pro bono case, sir, my expense. Will you follow me, Inspector Joyce?" Hettie said as she brushed by McCloud and opened the door to the elevator.

McCloud stood there not sure how to react.

Hettie could not really afford to do this case without pay. She just didn't want anybody to not have legal assistance.

"Thank you very much," Joyce said as the lift started moving up to the second floor.

Patrick looked at Hettie long and hard.

Then smiled.

"Did the hair every grow back on that patch on your head?"

Hettie's eyes went big. No one except Christina and Arnold knew about that.

She looked at Patrick.

"Do I know you, sir?"

"Not really. But I never forget the eyes and of course that flaming red hair was a sure giveaway."

Hettie looked at him a question mark all over her face.

"A farm way out in the Free state near Singers post. Your mom still alive?"

"Who are you?" Hettie said again.

"I'm the officer that gave you water after that bastard picked you up by the hair and threw you on the wagon."

"You're that officer?" she said.

"Patrick Murray at your service."

Hettie smiled. "I'm now Hettie Zimmer," she said. "Wonderful to meet you after all these years, Inspector. Never ever said thanks, was too frightened way back then. Thanks," she said.

"Was an honor and a pleasure."

"And your mom?"

"She's well, she is a granny now. I have a lovely little boy," Hettie said playing the part of a mother.

Joyce had no idea what was going on, and Murray explained it all to her.

The young girl explained what had happened, how she had been mugged and dragged off to a shack way out in the Langlaagte area. There she had been raped repeatedly and tortured for days.

Hettie never wavered; this amazed Murray.

She wrote down the facts and asked questions repeating them to make sure the answers were the same.

"Now do we have a suspect?" she asked Murray.

"We surely do."

"And he's in custody."

"No. As a matter of fact, he is out on five-hundred-pound bail."

"Must have a good attorney or rich friends."

"Must have," Murray said. "But I have a man watching him. Don't want him to get away."

"And his name?"

"Well, I think he's using an alias. He goes under the name of Barney Smith. We checked up on the documents, and they seem to tie up, but we have a difficult time getting any history on the man."

He took out his notebook:" Said he came over from Australia just as the war ended, worked odd jobs in Durban, made his way to Johannesburg to make his fortune.

Lives in Fordsburg. He is a loner, a bit of a thug, known to most as a loan shark, has some friends that follow him about. They probably paid his bail. We got hold of him when he tried to pawn Ms. Greenham's purse.

Claims he picked it up, but on searching his room where he lived found numerous items of other people as well as Joyce's briefcase. Joyce said she never lost it and had it with her the night she was kidnapped on her way home from the bank where she worked. That's all we have right now."

"Did you find the shack she described?"

"Not yet, but I have men out here looking for it. We know where she found help, so we have an idea where it might be, but with all the trees and various workout mines about, we are having a hard time."

"Well, Joyce, Patrick, I will set up a case as good as I can with what I have right now. Doesn't seem to be much, but we will try our best. Has any court dates been set up?"

"Not yet, but we will now be proceeding with that," Patrick answered.

When they were gone, the vivid memories of that day came back, and Hettie shivered.

She never contacted her mom to tell her about Patrick, didn't want to upset her in any way, so just let it be.

The case was flimsy. She had nothing that could place Joyce in Barney's presents. The rest was circumstantial at the moment. It was up to Murray to see if he could find some proof; otherwise she would have a hard time proving the case.

Joyce had identified Smith in a lineup.

And the fact that he was out there made her very frightened. Patrick Murray solved the problem by having her sleep in the police cells at night and making sure a constable walked with her to work and back.

A sandstone building that projected the law with a wide facade a domed roof and big columns that flanked the big arched entrance completed the picture.

Solicitor lawyers advocated and judges all in typical British court attire bustled about the interior.

South African law is based on the Dutch Roman law system. A judge rules and decides on evidence given. He then gives his verdict and punishment for the crime.

Advocates, lawyers, and solicitors presented their cases. For the defense or for prosecution and on evidence given and presented to the judge, a ruling and sentence is passed down.

Advocates normally handle serious cases like murder, rape, and attempted murder.

Although Hettie was not yet an advocate, she was deemed proficient enough by her company to represent and defend Joyce Greeham. The fact that she did it pro bono made the decision so much easier for the board members.

The court was not a large courtroom. It had the normal rows of seats for the public or students that wished to attend. A judge's seat was not the customary big pulpit type structure just a slightly raised big desk of sorts.

The whole inside of the court was covered with wood paneling with two large windows on one side. A single door at the back, a high ceiling with an enormous chandelier that lit up the proceedings. There was a small barrier that separated the judge from everybody.

"In the case of Ms. Joyce Greenham against Mr. Barney Smith, Judge Wilhelm Lodewick presiding.

The judge sat down and then spoke. "I have here a case of rape and abduction. Attorney Zimmer, you represent Ms. Greenham?"

"I do, your honor. Ms. Greenham, you state that on the night of the 1 of June 1922. Mr. Smith abducted you and then raped you consecutively while he tortured you. Is that correct?"

"That's correct."

"Is this the man that you identified as being the person alleged to have done these deeds?" he pointed at Smith.

"He is your honor."

"Will you rise, Mr. Smith?"

"Mr. Petrus Alberts, you represent Mr. Smith?"

"I do."

"What does your client plead?"

"He pleads not guilty, your honor."

"Is that correct, Mr. Smith?"

"Yes," Barney answered.

"We will convene here on the 24 June so that I can hear the case."

"Court sojourned."

Hettie watched long and hard. There was something about Barney Smith that she just couldn't place. Was it his walk or his eyes, she couldn't really tell as he wore those thick spectacles. Something told her she knew this man.

"Patrick, I know this man."

Strange you say that, but I also have a feeling I have met him somewhere before and that he is trouble.

Patrick was getting fed up with his people and the investigation.

"What have you found?"

"Nothing, sir, nothing at all."

He swore.

"Joyce, come."

As they stepped from his car, she felt the fear she had that day she had knocked on the door for help not knowing what to expect.

"Is this the house?"

"Yes."

"You came from which side?"

"That way."

It took Patrick less than thirty minutes to find the burnt-out ruins of shack.

"Dammit, he burnt it down."

"Want every piece of ruble checked and checked again. Anything that could remotely be evidenced must go in this bag."

"That's rotten luck," he said to Joyce, "but it does prove to a certain extent that what you've been saying is true."

They followed the path from the shack in the opposite direction, and it led to the outskirts of Fordsburg.

"We have nothing concrete at this point, but I am working my men hard to find something more concrete," he said to Hettie at court.

Joyce was asked to take the stand and then present her side of what had happen to her. The details were shocking and seemed unreal.

"I was walking home from work. It was about 5:00 p.m. on a Friday. I was going to stop at the small shop on the corner of Fifth Street and Seventh Avenue to buy some bread and some sliced cold meat to make me dinner.

When he asked if I would be so kind as to just show him how to get to the station."

"The he you are referring to," the judge asked, "can you point him out to me?" She pointed at Barney Smith.

"Proceed."

"He looked a kind, nice man, so I thought I would quickly show him it was on my way and would take a few short minutes."

"We walked, and then as we turned down Second Street, he grabbed me, pulled me into an alley, and knocked me over the head.

When I woke up, I was tied up, and in a shed of some sorts, I shouted for help. He was there and only laughed. He told me that we were miles from anywhere and that no one could hear me shout. Then he ripped off my clothes, sat back, and looked at me.

He told me he was going to enjoy raping me."

Joyce broke down and cried.

"Can we take a small break, your honor? It is obvious my client is in big distress."

"We will take a fifteen-minute recess."

Joyce returned a bit more composed.

"Ms. Greenham, will you proceed please?"

"He drank some brandy. I think that's what it smelt like."

Joyce was whimpering as she spoke.

"Are you okay, Joyce?" Hettie asked.

"No, no, I'm okay," Joyce said as she braced herself. "You sure?" Hettie asked again.

"Yes, yes," she waved Hettie off.

"Then he hit me hard in the face. Over and over again. I can't remember how many times I was bleeding from my mouth, then he lifted my head and kissed me, told me how he loved the taste of blood.

He got undressed and told me to look at him. I cried and pleaded that he wouldn't do anything to me, but all he did was laugh.

Then he grabbed my hair and pulled my head back hard, it was extremely painful, and proceeded to rape me while hurting me in every way he could."

She was crying now, and Hettie asked the judge to please call a halt.

The judge did.

"We will reconvene at 9:00 am tomorrow."

Joyce was shaking when Patrick and Hettie helped her back to her bench.

Barney and his lawyer brushed past again. Hettie felt that feeling she knew this man. She knew him, but her mind couldn't place where.

After making sure she had been given something to calm her, Joyce was taken to the cells were she felt safe.

They returned the next morning.

"Will you be able to continue?" Ms. Greenham

The court scribe read back the last few words of Joyce's statement.

"He had some more brandy and just left me there hanging and crying. I told him he had got what he wanted, to please let me go, I wouldn't tell anybody. He just smiled and said, "That's true, my dear, you will not.""

"He lit a cigar then burned me on my breast with the match."

Hettie stood up.

"Judge, we have here a photo taken by the police at the Fordsburg Police Station showing all Ms. Green's injuries. The first photo shows her breasts and the blisters."

The judge looked at the photos then placed it to one side.

"Then he got dressed and left."

"He left?" Hettie asked.

"Yes."

"Did he return?"

"Yes, but it was late in the afternoon, close to getting dark when he came back."

"Proceed."

"He had a box. In the box, he had red ants."

"Red ants?" Hettie asked.

"How do you know that?"

"The box was a glass box and had this hole in the top with leather all around it, then he came to me and said, 'you are going to enjoy this, dear.'

"He tied my foot to a heavy metal anvil so I couldn't move it.

"He undid a latch that opened the hole in the glass box, grabbed my foot, placed it in the box, and slammed it shut. It took the ants seconds before they started biting and eating my foot. I screamed in pain and tried to free myself but couldn't. Eventually the pain was too much, and I fainted."

"When I woke up, he had taken the box off, and my foot was just bare stripped of skin by the ants."

Hettie stood up and said, "That would be photos 3 to 8, your honor."

The judge looked at the photos. It was obvious he was shocked.

"Proceed," he said.

"Then he was gone. He never gave me water or food or anything. He came back later that day. He told me he wanted oral sex, and if I wasn't going to give him, he would place my other foot in the box with ants."

"I did it. I gave him what he wanted!" she almost screamed it when she said it.

"It's okay, Joyce, it's okay." Hettie calmed her down.

She composed herself.

"After he was satisfied that I had done what he wanted, he grabbed my other foot and tied it to the anvil and placed in the box with the ants laughing. I lied he said. I went thru the pain all over again until I couldn't take it no more. I wet myself and then fainted."

"When I woke up, he was gone, and my right foot had also been stripped off its skin by the ants."

Hettie rose. "That's photos 9 to 15, your honor." The judge never looked at the photos.

"Proceed."

"Did he return?" the judge asked this time.

"He did, your honor."

"When he came back, he never spoke to me. He just came in, grabbed me, and raped me again. Then he left. He never said a word."

"How long did this carry on?" Hettie asked Joyce.

"I lost count after five days."

"He had bought the same box with three rats in it and placed my hand in it so the rats could eat my hand."

"Photos 18 to 24," Hettie said.

"Can you show the judge your hand please, Joyce?" Hettie asked.

Joyce held up her hand that had been badly deformed.

"Proceed"

"He told me if I gave him one of my fingers, he would let me go. After he slowly cut off my finger with a knife, he laughed and said he lied. Again."

"Joyce, show your other hand to the judge."

She lifted her left hand, showing the pinkie missing.

"He loved burning me with hot pokers."

"Photos 24 to 35," Hettie said.

The case had attracted some attention from the press due to it being so horrible and shocking, but no one was allowed to photograph either Joyce or Barney.

"One evening he came in and took of all the chains and told me to sit down, then he opened the door. He took a gun and placed it on the table and sat down. He said that I could shoot him if I wanted or shoot myself whatever I choose. That way, I would be free."

"I took the gun, but I realized it was not loaded. It was one of his tricks again. My father was a gunsmith, so I knew when I couldn't see the shell casings in the chamber that it wasn't loaded."

"So instead of shooting at him, I threw the gun at him as hard as I could, but I missed and hit the paraffin lamp behind him that exploded and covered him in paraffin, so he started to burn."

"He jumped up to put out the flames. That's when I ran out the door he had left open. I ran down the path then climbed a tall tree where I hid."

"He came out looking for me swearing if he found me, he would make me pay dearly. I would have pain I wouldn't believe. I sat in the tree till the next day, climbed down, got some clothes, and ran till I came to some houses. They took me to the police station."

"Do you wish to add anything else, Miss Greenham."

"No, your honor."

"We will stand in recesses till 9:00 am tomorrow. Then Mr. Alberts, you can cross-examine if you so wish."

Christina had heard that Hettie was involved in serious court case that had everybody talking, so she wanted to see what it was all about and decided to make a trip to Johannesburg, visit Jonathan, then pop in at the court to see what the fuss was about.

It was early morning as she walked down Prichard Street.

As she turned the corner of Kruis and Prichard, she froze.

There walking across the road was Breton Winslow. Even though he had done his best to camouflage his appearance—he had glasses on, his hair was black—but his image had been burned into Christina's mind for life. No disguise, no makeup—nothing—would hide him from her ever. As he removed his glasses to wipe them, she saw his eyes.

She went white. Her eyes wide, magnifying his face. She could see those terrible eyes, those snakelike golden eyes. She felt ill. Christina started running although he was a good 150 yards away. She wanted to get to him and strangle the life out of him.

She stopped holding on to the tree on the sidewalk next to the lawn to the court where she vomited violently. An old man walked up to her. "Are you all right, madam?" he asked. She turned, and when he saw her eyes, he stepped back. "Must I call for help?"

"No." She waved him off. "Must be something I ate. I will be okay," she said.

"You're sure?"

"Yes, I am positive. Thanks."

She found a bench and sat down.

Winslow had disappeared into the courtroom.

She sat there for close on two hours then stood up and walked the opposite direction.

Hettie's case was falling apart. Everything Joyce said couldn't be proven. Nothing she said was found in the burnt shack. They needed more evidence, else Barney Smith was going to walk free.

Petrus Alberts tried to be soft with Joyce, never badgered her. He just asked simple yes-and-no questions.

"Do you have anything else you wish to present?"

"Yes, your honor, we have, but we need some time to get the facts straight so we can present it. Something new has been given to us. She held up a piece of paper."

"How much time?" the judge asked.

"About three weeks?" she asked.

"The court will reconvene in three weeks," Mr. Smith the judge turned to Barney. "Don't be foolish and try to run off. That would be a sure admission of guilt." With that, the judge retired to his office.

"You have something new?" Patrick asked.

"I have nothing, but unless we get something in the next three weeks, he will walk free."

What was the paper you showed the judge?" Patrick asked. "It's a flyer for woman's hats."

He laughed. "You're my kind of lawyer," he said.

Although Patrick worked hard asking every person he could, every contact he had, no one had seen Joyce in Barney's presence. Even if they had, it didn't count for much.

As they walked into court, Hettie knew she had lost, and this evil man was going to walk free.

The judge entered and sat down, was about to speak when Christina entered the courtroom. There was a short buzz from the people and press.

"Mrs. Venter," the judge said. "Good morning."

"Good morning, judge," Christina said. "Sorry for disrupting your court case."

"Not at all please."

Christina made her way to Hettie then sat down just behind her.

"Hi, Mom, what you doing here?"

"Just thought I would come and see what you're doing." Christina turned and looked straight at Barney Smith long and hard, put her hand to her mouth, and whispered something in Hettie's ear, then Patrick's ear. The all looked at Barney Smith.

He knew the game was up. This lady was in with the judge; if she said one word against him, he would hang.

He turned to his lawyer.

Jonathan had taken the bus in to town twice a week, snuck into the courtroom, asked one of the policemen to let him in one of the side rooms. Told him he was Hettie's son, but that he must please not tell his mother, then by looking thru a crack in the door. He had a good view of everybody.

Children were not allowed in the courtroom. He sat there with his pencil and paper drawing the judge, Barney Smith, Hettie with her black robe and white hairpiece, Patrick, and Joyce. The stuff that was said or talked about was never heard by him. His mind and eye were focused on the people, the faces, and the expressions.

He enjoyed it, but most of all, he enjoyed watching his mom doing something she truly loved and was extremely good at. He didn't want her to know he was there and would sneak out when it was over taking the bus back to Malvern where they lived on Park Street.

But he showed his dad. "Mom looks mean in her court attire," he said; they laughed.

"This is the bad guy."

"Yes, Dad. He looks evil, doesn't he, and this one, this is the lady they say he tortured."

"Yes."

"She's quite a good-looking lady." Jonathan hit his dad's arm. "Hey, Mom, will have your hide if you say that. They laughed again.

They heard Hettie coming up the stairs, so Jonathan hid his drawings, grabbed his math book, and made as thou he was studying.

"Hard day."

"Sure as hell," Hettie said as she turned her head so Arnold could kiss her on the cheek.

"Has anybody made food?"

"We sure have," Arnold said. "Chicken rice veggies."

"Will be down in a second, just want to take a bath. Can you bring a glass of wine if we have any left?"

"Yes, my dear, your wish is my command," Arnold said as he bowed.

Jonathan giggled.

After pouring her a tall glass of white chardonnay that was well chilled, he walked up stairs and knocked on the bathroom door.

The house was a small house because it was situated on the hillside. It seemed to have two levels, but actually, it was just one level staggered to compensate for the angle of the hill.

There was a small lounge with a fireplace, a sofa, two armchairs, a coffee-table, and a showcase that housed brick and brack that was important to Hettie. A short passage led to a kitchen with a large coal stove, black with chrome fittings, a wooden fridge that had a holder for the ice block at the bottom, and to the right was a small pantry. The back doors opened to a narrow passage that housed trash cans and a holder for wood and coal.

"Come in," she said. Hettie lay in the bathwater that had some soapsuds on the water but not enough to cover her naked body. "Your wine, madam."

Opposite the lounge across the passage, a dining room was situated. A table, four chairs, ball, and claw in red rosewood. With a welsh dresser showing some plates on it shelves. Tapestries hung behind glass in frames on the wall mostly made by people Hettie new back home.

Coming out the dining room and turning left, you would find the staircase next to that a door that lead to the downstairs toilet.

As you exit the stairs, there was a landing all round with two doors, one leading to Hettie's and Arnold's bedroom, the other to Jonathan's room—the window's lookout over the houses opposite and to Jule's street with its trams, the mines, and the dumps behind that.

To the back was a storage room; next to that, the bathroom and upstairs toilet.

Hettie had a magnificent body—full breasts, shapely hips, muscled legs, flat belly. He looked at her longing, would have loved to just climb in the bath with her, and make passionate love with her; but she hardly noticed he was there.

"Bloody case is going nowhere. He's going to walk free, Arnold. I am telling you I am going to lose this case I have nothing."

"I am sure it will work out, you'll see. I know you'll find something."

"Hope your bloody right," she said. "Else I am going to look like a complete idiot, and that bastard is going to be free."

She stood up. "Give me the towel, please," she said. Arnold found it hard not to stare, but even if he did, Hettie wouldn't have noticed. She was way too tied up in her thoughts.

Arnold was hard, so hard he could hardly walk, but said nothing. He knew it would lead to an argument, and she would blame him and nothing would happen. And he knew she would go to sleep still mumbling about her court case.

They ate. She asked the polite questions to Jonathan, "How was school? How are you doing? Are you studying? Have you done all your homework?"

Arnold said he would do the dishes. She retired to the lounge with her second glass of wine, put on an All Jolsen record, kicked up her feet, and sat back.

As he washed and dried the dishes, Arnold and Jonathan were planning a trip to the Wemer pan. They had read an article by the Turfontein Piscatorial society that someone had his line broken by a monster fish. The writer thought that it could be a big carp or barble (catfish).

Jonathan went to have a bath. Arnold went to sit in the lounge. Hettie sat on the armchair opposite him. She had on the bathrobe she had put on when she came down for dinner. As she sat, her naked her legs slightly apart, her eyes closed listening to the record. Arnold could see her natural red pubic hair. It aroused him all over again. He tried not to look but couldn't help himself.

She woke up and saw him looking. "Come on, man, please none of that. I am tired, had a long day. Dammit, don't you ever stop." She took her wine and disappeared upstairs.

Arnold sat there. He loved her more than anything in the world. He loved her the moment he had seen her at the ball, that's why he noticed she didn't have a necklace.

But as time went on in their marriage, she seemed less and less attracted to him. Occasionally she would come into the bedroom, undress, and say, "We better do it else you'll be hounding me like a dog after a bitch. Do it she would say."

It was something Hettie knew was wrong. She hated being this way but just could not stop herself.

As she walked up the stairs, she stopped for a brief second. Him looking at her, desiring her even though she's been really mean to him made her feel guilty. She thought of going back and saying let's do it, then she said no to herself and went upstairs to turn in.

Arnold would just have to satisfy himself. I gave him enough to make that easy, she thought.

Arnold sat there for a long while. The record made that click-switch-click sound as it had reached its end. What was he doing wrong? What had he done wrong? Why did she hate him like she did? There never was any answer and never would be. Then he said to himself, "Dammit, if I only didn't love her that much."

Christina leaned over to Hettie. "That man is not Barney Smith. It's Breton Winslow." Hettie looked at him and saw immediately what she had recognized. She was shocked.

Patrick asked what it was, and she told him. "Shit," he said, "was the glasses. If he taken them off, I would have known. I had seen him before. He's as guilty as sin, that one, wish we had more against him." They were all looking at Winslow.

Winslow (Barney) turned to his lawyer. "Who's the lady behind Mrs. Zimmer?" "Oh, that's Hettie's mother, Mrs. Christina Venter. That is one lady you wouldn't want on your wrong side. Her husband is the third richest man in Africa, if not the world. It is estimated that his net worth is in the region of twenty-five million pounds. Hope she has nothing to add to the case. If she as much as whispers anything to the judge, we are done, my friend. I can tell you that you will be hanged." He smiled at Winslow as though he was joking. Winslow sat down. The judge was just about to ask Hettie if she had any more to add when Winslow jumped up to his lawyer's amazement.

"I want to change my plea to guilty but on a lesser charge of attempted rape."

The judge turned and looked at Petrus Alberts. "Are you still representing your client, Mr. Alberts?"

"I am, your honor. Could I just consult with my client for a second please?"

"What do you think you're doing?" he asked.

"I know a bit about the law. If I plead guilty to a lesser charge, I might walk away with say eight or ten years of jail time. But if I am convicted, I will be hanged."

"They have nothing," Petrus said. "They actually have a lot," Winslow said. "Will tell you later, please, enter my plea."

"You absolutely sure what are you not telling me?"

"I am."

Petrus rose and said, "My client wants to plead guilty on a lesser charge of attempted rape. He feels that because he had tried to rape Ms. Greenham. She had manufactured this horrendous story to get back at him and see him hang."

"Is this true, Mr. Smith?"

"It is, your honor."

Joyce jumped up. "He's a liar. He raped me, your honor, he is lying!" "Attorney Zimmer, control your client." Hettie asked Joyce to sit down. "He is lying," was all Joyce said. "He is lying."

"We have nothing, Joyce. If we pursue, he walks free and will get back at you. Him pleading guilty is the best you will get."

Joyce was shaking.

"Give us a moment, your honor." Hettie said.

Christina leaned over to Hettie. "Take the guilty plea."

"What?" she said to her mother. "Take the plea," her mother had the chill and depth of an iceberg in her voice.

Hettie looked at her mom and could see that her mom was white, eyes black. She turned slowly to face the judge.

"I have spoken to my client although she feels she is not lying and due to the lack of concrete proof we will accept the plea."

"In that case, Mr. Albert's, I will proceed with sentencing after the noon hour break. Mr. Smith will be taken into custody until such time. Court sojourned till twelve-thirty."

Joyce was still crying. Christina came around and took Joyce in her arms. "Come with me." "Mom," Hettie protested. But she saw that look and backed off.

Christina, with Joyce by her side, disappeared into the hallway of the court.

"Knew. I knew the bastard." Patrick stood up and walked over to Winslow.

"Why change your name, Mr. Winslow?"

Winslow (Barney) looked at Patrick.

Patrick leaned over and took of his glasses.

"Now there we are. Yes, yes, there are those snake eyes."

"Inspector Murray, I would ask you to refrain from calling my client names."

"Listen," he said looking at Petrus, "this bag of dog shit can be glad he pleaded guilty because I would have loved to have had him walk free outside, would have loved that," he said in a voice that would make a demon cringe.

He threw the glasses back at Winslow, turned, and walked back to Hettie.

"Is there any way we can use the crimes he did in the war against him?"

"I don't think so. The government would not want to see a British soldier stand trial. It would result in a big political debacle. They will not allow that to happen."

"Well, my dear, it seems we got a bitter victory of sorts. Would have loved to have seen the bastard struggle with a rope strung around his neck."

"So would I," Hettie said.

When Christina and Joyce returned, Joyce was actually smiling.

"Your okay, Joyce?" Hettie asked.

"Never felt better."

"You sure?" She turned to her mom.

"Don't look at me," her mom said. "I just tried to make her feel good."

"She did," Joyce said with a small smile.

"All rise." The judge entered.

"Will the accused please rise?"

"To be honest, Mr. Smith, if I could have my way, I would like to see you pay the full price for what you've done to this poor lady. But this is the law, and the law only bases its findings and sentencing on facts and proof. But that does not mean that I cannot give you what you justly deserve."

I sentence you to ten years in jail without any chance of parole whatsoever."

"Bailiff see that Mr. Smith is taken away to Pretoria maximum prison where he will start his sentence."

As the bailiff was walking out, Christina stood up and looked at Winslow as he came past. He smiled at her then laughed.

When Hettie got home that evening, she was happy yet very upset all at the same time.

She baled away to Arnold about how this man should have hung, but he's free because she didn't have enough evidence. If she could just have found something, she could have had this demon of a man hung. She had him in her grasp, but he got free. "Fuck," she said. "Watch your language," Arnold said. "We still have a kid in the house." "Sorry," she said.

"Come, sit down," he said. "Relax. It's over. It's not like he's free. He is in jail. He is not out there, at least that's a blessing. And you haven't lost the case. You actually won with limited evidence at that."

"I know, I know. It's just him. Winslow. He's the devil incarnate." She hit the kitchen table.

Late that evening, Arnold had her lay down so he could rub her back and take the tension out of her body. He gave her a massage. With as much love and care as he could muster, making her feel good, when she turned on him. She basically raped him. She fell on the bed completely exhausted. Arnold lay there stunned. The sex was good, but she was possessed as thou she wanted to hurt him, not give him pleasure.

They had the drawn pictures in the paper of Barney Smith/Breton Winslow. But they were at best mediocre. After looking at them, Arnold took Jonathan's pictures and went down to the *Daily Mail*. It took but a few seconds for even the newspaper court artists to exclaim that this was as good as a black-and-white photograph of the accused and all those present.

With ten pounds in his pocket, he returned home, and when Jonathan came home from school, he handed him the *Daily Mail* for the evening. Jonathan sat there speechless paging thru the paper, looking at his own drawings now in print. Oh, and by the way, young man, that Mitchell fishing real you wanted so much, here is the ten pounds the newspaper paid me for your drawings?"

Jonathan was jumping about the kitchen.

They heard Hettie coming in and composed themselves. And went back to pretending to be doing something while doing nothing.

"Well, that was an uneventful day. What's this about me being in the mail? Mrs. Holmes says there's a photo of me in the mail."

She took the newspaper and started looking at the pictures. Arnold put his hand on his mouth showing Jonathan to be quiet.

"Not bad whoever the artist was. He is damn good if I have to say so. He got Winslow spot-on. As for me, I don't know, do you think that looks like mommy?" She showed the picture to Jonathan.

"No, no, that doesn't look like you," he said. "It's close thou," she said. "Very close." Closed the newspaper and went upstairs. When she was gone, they burst out laughing.

CHAPTER 7

Leaving Bloemfontein was the only way out. If the Boer men returned and heard what he had done, no British army would save him. He laughed. "There is going to be some seriously pissed-off men when they get back to the camp." Telling me," Patrick Peal said. "Especially that one we screwed and now she's pregnant, that's gone to take some explaining."

They laughed again. "Let's make dust, guys. We have to get as far as possible from this place as we can, and may I add let's never return." He smiled.

A thick cloud of smoke hung over the city. The smell of mine chemicals hung in the air like floating dandy lions.

It's the way things are in life, that people would migrate to others that have their same morals and way of life. Those attractions lead them to Ferreira's town.

Like swans gliding on a lake, they sailed in as thou they were always there. With the cream of life's scum was like being at home to them.

Winslow's cruel nature quickly got him the nickname Hurt. His reputation also made him a person to be feared and to steer clear of. Local prostitutes would quickly scamper away leaving only those that would sell even their own souls for money. Money needed by them to buy the opium and morphine they required to face each day.

The small room he had was all he required. The jewels, watches and money that were stolen from the wife's, they took to the camps, were now the bounty and treasure they lived on.

Although there were some hard men in this part of town, they quickly realized that to Winslow, it was never about strength or power. No, it was about pain and cruelty, and he would have the toughest man begging for mercy by inflicting pain beyond their imagination, always befriending them then pouncing like a scorpion with its sting ready to strike.

The man playing cards with them was laughing and joking till Winslow shoved a knife thru his hand into the table. He screamed and tried to get up, but as he placed his other hand on the table, Winslow thrust a knife thru that hand as well, leaving him pinned to the table. That was when Winslow would do his work to everybody's entertainment. Burning cutting tearing the man's ears of one at a time. Until the man had no option but to break free from his situation ruining his hands in the process and fleeing. The scum of this part of town would know this was no man to tangle with ever. He had no friends, only victims. Even Patrick and Donald knew that they themselves had been cruelly hurt by him but stayed with him out of fear.

The man he had on the chair his eyes bulging as he gasped for air with Winslow having a very thin string around his neck looked at Winslow then he went limp and died.

Winslow wanted to make it as nothing, but a death was a death. He had about fifty witnesses, and he knew that all of them would love to see him hang. As people fled the scene, he knew he was in big trouble. Ran to his room, took all his belongings, and fled south to Durban He had walked all night until he came to Jeppe station, there he had caught a train that would take him south. "Listen, guys, you need to get out of town," he said to Patrick and Donald. "Go, do your own thing for a while. We will meet up later."

"You being with me will make you accomplices and easy for them to catch up to us. If we split up, it will be difficult to find us. "They agreed but thought to themselves, *If they catch us, we will gladly tell them where you are, the two men ventured south as well.*

They quickly started running short of cash and money. The two started there raping murdering and thieving spree in the southern part of the Free State. When they saw Christina in town, Patrick recognized her. It was when Mr. Cohen had said, "Well, if you need anything, Mrs. Venter, just call."

"I will," then he added, "when will Danny be back?"

"O, only in about five day's time, take care," she said.

That was their cue. It was Donald's idea that they don't get into a fight with her again but have her come to them. They just kidnap the daughter then she would do what they wanted. Patrick disagreed and said she will not do anything unless she knew the kid was safe. So what do you suggest? That's when they came up with their plan to have Hettie standing on a barrel with a hangman's noose around her neck far away where Christina could see her and out of reach. While Donald had his way with her, then Patrick and then they would do the daughter, shoot both, loot the farm, and be off.

"Why don't we screw them and get it over with?" "No, my friend, this bitch owes me and owes me big time. She will give me whatever I want and give it to me, no fighting no screaming. She's even going to say she loves me and loves being with me." He laughed.

They had never reckoned with Christina, and both died that same day.

Winslow found himself in Durban amongst people that viewed life exactly like he did and never flinched at anything he did but would easily sell their liver for two pennies, just for the hell of it.

The poster on the wall outside the post office left no doubt that it was him and that he was wanted. It never stated a reward but said that there might be a reward for information of his whereabouts.

In a back room on the docks, he hooked up with the man they called the Wizard, known to get whatever people needed or wanted. Winslow needed a new identity and quick.

With black hair, fake glasses, a suit, bowler hat and forged birth certificate and identification papers, Breton Winslow became Barney Smith.

He prowled around Durban for just over a year doing petty crimes, swindling, pimping. He kept himself out of harm's way, and when the war came stayed in the shadows even developed a limp so as to make that he was medically unfit for service.

As soon as the war was over, he made his way back to Johannesburg. As the train pulled in to Johannesburg station, Winslow felt he was home. Made his way down to Ferreira's town and worked the outskirts of Sophia town, a black township.

In the pit of life's despair where the debris of life floats about. when one piece of debris disappears, no one notices and no one cares.

He found an old miner's shack way of the beaten track. Made it his little den. This was the place where he could satisfy his eternal hunger for misery and pain in others.

Kidnapping men and woman from the fringes of life was easy. Then he would bring them to his den and have his way with them in the most heinous way imaginable. Till they would eventually reach that point where killing themselves would be the only way out, that was his moment of ultimate power to get someone to that point where he would leave himself totally at their risk. No arms, no weapons, even sometimes turned his back on them but knowing full well that his power was supreme, and they would then take their own lives. Numerous old mine shafts some hundreds of feet deep were ideal disposable sites for his victims.

As he walked down station road, there was a big ball going on. He stopped and looked with disdain and hate at those that lived the high life. The lady at the window looked elegant in her evening dress. "Fucken rich people, hate you!" he spat on the ground. He turned the corner and walked off.

Winslow was a young boy with white hair, born of very rich parents, his father an earl, the earl of Winthrop. At an early age, he was taken under the wing by his grandfather. A mean man, an evil character. Had the small boy, barely three, wring chickens neck, cut sheep's throats, butcher them, take out their guts. He laughed when the boy got sick doing it. The boy changed and started to enjoy the blood and gore. Loved the pain the animals went thru. He started abusing the animals on the farm except his dad's horses. The only thing his father cared about. Once he did hurt a horse, his father made him crawl on the ashes. Like a common servant for that. At twelve years old, he raped one of the chambermaids, threatened her with death. As he walked in the stable, saw her hanging there, he ran, his hand way up her dress as though she was alive and laughed. "You like that, don't you?" His cruelty and abuse of the staff continued. When it became such a problem that the local constabulary threatened action, his father loaded him in a carriage one day took him and enrolled him into the British army. Winslow loved the whole idea of war guns hurting, people shooting people. Would sit for hours listening to the cruelty of some stories soldiers told. Then he was posted to Cape Town, South Africa, when talk of the war came.

As with most soldiers that were permanent force, they were given rank. He became Sgt. Breton Winslow.

From Cape Town to Bloemfontein where he recruited the cream of lives evil vomit.

The assignment to round up women and children from the farms was like honey to a bagger. They partook of the carnage and slaughter, rape, and thieving like they were attending holy communion.

It never stopped for Winslow. It was a drug that he needed people had to suffer. Deep inside, it made the suffering he endured bearable as others also suffered.

Winslow's only problem was he hated pain himself. Feared it as he did when he was a kid and his father took a whip to him.

Joyce was a big mistake. He only realized that she wasn't a prostitute or a loner but someone everybody knew when the bag he had back at his shack showed she worked at the bank.

As he sat there day after day in court, he felt good. He had triumphed, not even the law could catch him.

That was until he saw Christina. She was the one that never gave in. He tried hard. He did everything he could, but the bitch as he called her wouldn't give up. She had grown older, looked different with her hair all up in a bun, and with her elegant dress. But those eyes, he would know them amongst a thousand people.

He asked Petrus who she was, but he already knew.

———

"Mrs. Venter. Now there is one powerful lady, my friend. Don't cross her or be on her wrong side. I sat as a clerk once, and she got up to say what she had seen when a young man stole a handbag from an old lady knocking her down.

"It was a petty crime, would have probably got off with about one year in jail. After she spoke and her pull with the judge, he can be glad he only got three years. I thought the judge was going to hang him. Remember my boss Louis Turpin said to him, don't let her get in the stand, just plead guilty, you will get a small sentence and be out in a year. No, the young man was tough and was going to show her. Well, I think he thinks different now."

Winslow had listened to what Petrus had said. He knew full well if Christina got in the stand to tell her friend, the judge, who he really was, what he had done in the camps. A full investigation would be launched, he would be caught out, his papers weren't that foolproof, and he would get hanged, that was for sure.

He jumped up and asked to plead guilty to attempted rape. They didn't have any proof and chances are good that the prosecution lawyer would take it. That way he would get a prison sentence.

That's what happened

As he sat there in the room at the prison with a big prison guard in attendance, Christina Venter walked in.

"Look who's here, just to see me." He smiled. "Would love to get up but not for you."

She sat down.

"You think you're great. You think you are above the law, Winslow. But in this jail, you'll rot. For ten years, I tell you, it will give you enough time to think of the crimes, murders, and rapes you committed."

Winslow watched her did not even take a breath.

"Well, lady, it's like this. Prison is okay. First off all, if the Boer men knew who I was and how I enjoyed myself with their children, wives, and mothers, they would surely take my life. Here I am safe. No one can touch me. In no time, I will set up a network, have a music box, books, good food, even some wine, have the prison guards at my beck and call, and who knows be out of here for good behavior in five or, maybe, six years."

"You bastard," Christina said.

"I might be, lady," he said and laughed, "Damn, I should have taken you if it wasn't for that damn officer. You would have been perfect. Can see it in my mind's eye." He lay back. "You see, Mrs. Venter, with all your money and pull, I still win, you lose," then he laughed his evil laugh. Christina stood up, fuming. She threw the chair back and walked to the door.

Hettie went in to work even thou it was Saturday. She wanted to get some stuff organized she said to Arnold and Jonathan. She lied. She would rather work than be with the two of them.

"It's okay, Mom. Me and dad will be off to Wemmerpan, see if we can catch that big carp or barbell. Want to see if it's true. Just a pity the local hardware store didn't have any Mitchell reels, would have loved to take one with me. No fish would have gotten away if I had a Mitchell."

"Enjoy yourselves," she said leaving without a kiss or a hug.

"Mrs. Zimmer."

"Yes," she said to a man that had a big camera hanging around his neck.

"Please no photographs. I need to go to work. The case is over. Please, just leave me alone."

She turned and started up the steps leading to the big doors of the building.

"Actually," the voice said behind her, "wanted to know if you can get your son to do some drawings for us of the Clinton case."

She stopped and turned.

"What are you blabbering about?"

"Well, my editor was so impressed by the drawings of the Barney Smith case. He wanted to know if we can have him draw the Clinton case for us?"

Hettie froze. "Are you okay, ma'am?"

She nearly fell as she missed a step.

She composed herself, then said, "You say my son drew the court pictures of the Barney Smith case, the ones that was in the newspaper?"

"Sure did, ma'am. The daily news paid him ten pounds for those."

She faltered as she spoke. "What happened to the originals?" she said.

"Oh, they might be somewhere at the newspaper office," he said.

"I will be in my office. I will pay you twenty pounds if you can let me have those back."

"Sure thing," he said. "Do you think your son would be able to draw for us?"

"Will ask him," she lied. The young man was gone.

As she sat there looking at the drawings Jonathan had made, she started to cry bitterly. Her son had been in court, had drawn her, and she didn't even know.

She even said it didn't quite look like her.

"Mom." she said in the mouth piece of the phone.

"Yes, Hettie."

"I need to talk to you right now."

"Hettie, is everything okay?"

"No, it's not."

"What's wrong?"

"Just meet me at the African Pavilion. Please, Mom, in an hour please."

As Christina walked up to the table were Hettie sat, she could see that Hettie was a mess physically and emotionally.

She blabbered on to her mom about Jonathan and the drawings, that she was a bad mother, a cold wife, a useless attorney, sobbing and crying as she spoke.

Christina held her but never said a word.

"Hettie, the war, the camps—it made us hard and bad people without feelings. We saw way too many hurt and death every day. But we can't bring them back. We can't make right what was wrong."

"Yes, Mom, but now I could have had that pig Winslow hung, and I was not good enough to even do that."

"Just one second, lady." Christina shook Hettie violently.

"Even if you had proof, he would have still gotten ten years."

"No, Mom, he would have hung."

"No, Hettie, he would have gotten ten years. Nothing you said or did would change that."

Hettie looked at her mom. "What do you mean?"

"I'm going to tell you something. You never heard this from me. You never spoke to me, you never even knew anything about what I'm about to tell you. Are we clear?"

"What are you talking about, Mom?"

"Just listen to what I am about to tell you and swear to me you will never ever talk about this ever."

"What is it, Mom?"

"Swear to me, Hettie. Not Arnold no one"

Hettie wasn't sure what was happening.

"Swear," Christina held her by her shoulders.

"I swear, Mom."

"When I went to see you in court one day, I saw Breton Winslow entering the court. I went mad, wanted to get to him, and kill him with my bare hands. But I was running toward him when I stopped and realized. If he was to die, it would be over in a second for him."

"While you were trying to get Joyce justice, I went to Petrus Albert's law firm. I contacted him and found out that he had been in the camps as well." Hettie's eyes went big.

Her mom told her to be quiet.

"I instructed him to what I wanted him to do, to get Winslow to plead guilty the day I walked into that courtroom."

"Mom, you didn't," Hettie said.

Christina just held up her hand.

"When Petrus heard of what the evil Breton had done and who he really was, how evil and violent he was, how he murdered, raped, and killed—that he was a demon in disguise, he agreed to help me."

Christina held up her finger again.

"Petrus told her that he was from Standerton, was a victim himself of the camps, was locked up with his mother and sister. His sister had been raped, beaten, and then shot by the soldiers. His mother died in his arms when he was an eleven-year-old boy because someone had poisoned her food.

"I explained to him why it was important that Winslow pleaded guilty.

"Then I went to the judge whose wife was a good friend and patron of one of my welfare societies.

"I told the judge that I was tired of seeing men hung and killed like that. That the war was over and that if this man was indeed as evil as they said, that I and my husband who was a very, very rich man would be so glad if he was to get a long prison sentence. We would gladly support the judge when he wanted to be elected to parliament."

Hettie protested, "Mom, you didn't."

"Shh . . . listen to my story. I am never ever going to talk about this again, so listen carefully."

"Mom, this stuff is illegal. You shouldn't have done this."

"Don't you think I know that you're an attorney? That what I am telling you could ruin your career for life? I am fully aware of it and that's why I had you swear to me you wouldn't tell anybody ever."

"So I went to court knowing full well, that if Breton saw me, he might just recognize me and fall into the plan I had set up. He did, and Petrus played his part perfectly.

"Breton got ten years. You had no idea what was happening, and you couldn't have known. So you felt bad you had lost the case. As I told you, you never lost. If I had got up there and spoken against Winslow, he would have been dead by now. But him pleading guilty was the last piece of my plan."

Hettie was stunned.

"The day after the hearing, I went to Winslow, where he had been taken to Pretoria prison, and sat down to talk to him. I told him how I hated him, told him that I hoped he rotted in prison. But all he did was laugh and say he was going to have a ball once he had his network set up music, wine, good food, and he laughed his evil laugh."

She held her finger in the air when Hettie wanted to say something.

"I stood up, threw my chair back, and walked to the door of the room. Then I laughed aloud and from my heart."

"How was my acting"

"Winslow was shocked. 'What seems to be so funny?' he asked me.

"'You don't know, don't you?' I said.

"'I wanted you to get ten years.'

"Winslow looked at me. His snake eyes very unsure. Let me tell you why. Over here, this man standing there—I pointed at the guard—that's Lambert. Lambert's mom died when she tried to defend herself when a British soldier tried to rape her at the Irene concentration camp. I stood up and opened the door. 'Come in,' I said. A lot of people entered the room."

"Over here is Gert Knoetze, the prison warden. His sister and brother died while he was in the concentration camp at Stillfontein. Here we have Fanus Britz, the chaplain. Fanus lost his finger in Bloemfonatein when an evil man cut his finger off so he could get a bread for his mother."

"Winslow jumped up. 'You can't do this. I want my lawyer. I demand my lawyer,' he said. Petrus entered. Meet Petrus. His sister was raped and shot his mother poisoned at Bronkhorstspruit camp. Winslow wanted to protest some more, but Lambert hit him hard in the face. 'Now look at that,' I said. 'You're bleeding'."

"'Meet Anna. Anna was also in Bloemfontein Concentration Camp. See how her hand had been badly burnt. Some bad person poured boiling hot tea over her hand.'

"Anna came forward and placed some bad stuff on his busted lip that made it bubble."

"Oh, dear, I might have taken the wrong bottle. She said this looks like acid."

"By now, Winslow's eyes were popping out his head. I introduced him to everybody in the section. I had made sure that every guard, cleaner, nurse, chaplain, even the warden that had, had someone killed or murdered in the concentration camps or on the farms where they lived, was there.

"Winslow was frantic. 'You can't do this. The law will not allow this. Prisoners have rights,' he said.

"My answer was simple. 'Now you know all about prisoners and their rights now, don't you?' I still pinched his cheek when I said that. I know that's mean. Winslow tried to explain, even tried to say that we had the wrong person."

"I reminded him that he had owned up when we were alone that he knew me, even wanted so much to rape me. Winslow tried to get away, but the guards held him down. Just then, the door opened and Patrick Murray walked in."

"'Sorry I'm late. Did I miss the best part? 'Afraid you did.' I told him what happened.

"'Well, snake eyes, this time you're in for it, aren't you? I enjoyed when they hung shit bags like you, but man must tell you this here is the best ever. Now this is justice in all its glory.' I stepped over to Winslow and looked deep in to that snake eyes of his. Welcome to ten years of hell. 'You will for the next ten years get what you've been dishing out to helpless woman, children, men, and animals. You think what you did was painful, you think what you did was evil. These people lived that evil, and they want to return the favor. Anna will work day and night to keep you alive. Nobody wants you dying in here now, do they? Ten years, the warden will say, you're very bad and sometimes crazy. You will not be allowed any visitors whatsoever. Watch out what you eat though you never know. And I hear there are some men here that want to know you better in a personal way.'

"I turned to leave then stopped and came back. 'I will be here the day you are set free after ten years. With the newspapers, making sure that everybody will know who and what you really are, what you did in the camps, then we will let you face the people outside.'

"I laughed. So did everybody else, and I left. Now I'm going. Don't say a word. Don't ask me a thing. I told you a story. That's all, a story. And don't ever say you should have done better in court. You did your part perfect."

Christina kissed Hettie on the forehead then left.

Hettie sat there, and when the waiter came and asked if he could get her something, she said brandy neat. She suddenly realized that she had been part of a big plan. A plan to bring an evil monster the justice he deserved. That at this moment, thousands of victims were cheering.

As the burden of years of guilt fell off her like dead leaves, she wanted just one thing. She found them. They were sitting at a clear spot between some reeds.

"Mom?"

Jonathan looked surprised, not sure how to react. "I heard there was a young artist that was trying to catch a big carp here at this lake. Maybe if he used this Mitchell real, it would help. She held out a box to him. He jumped up—a Mitchell. He opened the box. "Look, Dad, and it even has line on it. Wow. That carp out there is as good as dead."

"Hey," Hettie said, "Doesn't your mom get a big kiss and hug?"

As he hugged her and kissed her, Hettie realized how much she had lost out on. "I also have here some nice ham and cheese sandwiches, some cold drink, six ice cold beers, and six custard slices. Is there a place for a cold-blooded woman to sit here somewhere?" she asked Arnold. He looked at her a big question mark on his face.

He patted the spot on the blanket next to him.

She sat down. Jonathan had reeled in his old line and placed his new Mitchell on the rod.

Hettie leaned over to Arnold.

"I was lost, Arnold. I was totally lost, in a forest of guilt, hate, and fear. Today I was set free." She was crying. "And when I was free," her voice broke, "I realized I wanted so much not to be free but to be with you. I love you and I'm so sorry. I am sorry for what I have done to you and Jonathan."

Jonathan cast in his line. It went for miles, even Arnold was amazed.

"Holy cow," he said, "that must be at least a hundred yards."

"I know this reel is fantastic." He placed it on the rests then came over and gave Hettie another hug. "Thanks, Mom, it's perfect."

"Let me put my marker on the line and see if I can catch that carp."

Arnold had his arm around Hettie. He held her very tight. She slipped her hand between his legs and squeezed him. He looked at her, his eyes big, then she whispered, "I'm not wearing any underwear." She giggled.

Christina knew that Danny was at the main bizzley at Hamilton in Bloemfontien. The South African marksman competition.

She had never ever gone back there after the war. She was scared of the memories.

"If we leave now, when can we be in Bloem?" She asked her guard.

"Well, if we drive right thru the night, I would say about ten or eleven tomorrow."

"Let's go."

"What about clothes and stuff, ma'am?"

"We will buy what we both need when we get there."

The monument with its cenotaph and the memory wall with all the names did not make Christina feel sad. She new some of the names, and as she walked down the wall, she kept saying aloud, "We got him. We got the devil and he's in hell right now. We got him. We got him!" She was happy. It was as if she could hear the voices and the cheers of those now dead many years shouting with joy.

They parked the car at the shooting range. She entered the back of the big hall like a structure that had no walls on the side.

Men were sitting everywhere. Most of them had rifles. The shooting range was off to the side, the big targets still out there—the furthest at one thousand yards. The man talking in front stopped.

"Gentleman. I am honored to present to you, Mrs. Christina Venter, the best markswoman/man in South Africa if not the world."

Danny came over to kiss her. "What are you doing here, came to see what the fuss was about?" She smiled.

Mr. Chairman—a young man decked out in a shooting jacket pads and holding a handmade German WW1 Sniper rifle. 762 bore with scope—spoke.

"You say this lady's is the best marksman/woman that South Africa has ever seen if not the world."

"Dead right, young man."

"Danny, you have the coins."

"Sure." Danny handed the speaker the coins.

The man held the three coins that were in a cellophane bag in the air. "These coins were shot with a standard, 303 open sites. At two hundred yards, this one at 225, and this one 250. One bullet each, no test shots in rapid succession, a feat not yet repeated."

The young man did not sit down. "That's all fair and well, sir, but no offense to anybody and at least to Mrs. Venter, but was anybody here there that day, or was it only her close friends? Further to that, I just shot a near perfect round all distance up to one thousand yards missing one shot by a hairs breath. Now that's a feat that is going to be hard to duplicate."

Danny stood up. It was obvious he was cross. "I was there. You calling me a liar?"

Christina spoke.

"Danny, sit down. Your name, young man?" Christina said.

"My name is Willem."

"Willem, I will tell you what. You know you are right, I agree with you I have been living my whole life with people doubting what I had done. I can't blame them except for my husband. No one else is here today to back up what had happened.

"But if the men here and you will allow me, I just want it to be clear what this shot was about. How difficult it really was. Nobody here has actually seen what a coin looks like at two hundred yards.

So we can all be clear on what the shots entailed, would you be so kind as to take—" She shuffled in her bag then stopped for a long time. "You okay, Christina?"

"Yes."

"Will you take this watch then ride out to four hundred yards then hold it like this?" She showed him to hold it between his thumb and finger. "Then I want everybody here to look thru their binoculars and telescopes and tell me what they see. I am aware that this is not a coin, but it's the same size and it's shinier. Want you to look thru your binoculars and telescopes. Tell me what it says on the watch. If you can see the markings on the watch, tell me what they say.

"If you can't, we will come closer. Once all can see it, we can then stop and determine the distance, and then everybody can make a sound judgment.

"If someone was shooting at something like this watch, the same size as a half-crown, surely they would have to see it clearly. Don't we all agree?"

"Would that be okay? I just want this to end, want these men to make a sound judgment so I can get some rest. How difficult this shot really was then you all can even try and shoot it once we agree on the distance, okay."

Everybody agreed. Willem and his friend jumped in a small Austin car and drove all the way to the 440-yard mark then got out the car. "Now please, this is important," she said. "I want everybody to look and see if they can see the watch and the marking. If not, we will wave him closer, okay? I only need one person to say he can see the marking."

All eyes were on the young man standing with the watch between his thumb and forefinger.

As they watched, even Danny looking thru his binoculars, you could hear them say, "Dammit, that is far. I can hardly see the watch much less the marking, can you?"

A single shot rang out. Willem felt a small tug as the watch disappeared from his hand; then the sound of the shot came to him, and he jumped back.

There was a long silence. Danny looked at Christina as she stood there with his 303 in her hand. No scope, just a plain old.303.

"Think that does it," she said. "Tell that little shit what is left of the watch is behind that white marker about 20 yards behind him."

She turned and said to Danny, "Let's go. It's a long way home."

As she looked down the barrel of the riffle, nothing had ever been magnified so clear in her life.

"Ma'am," the prison guard said, "maybe you'd like this as a memento" as he gave her the watch.

"Thanks." She had thrown it in the bag without a glance.

Breton Winslow. The inscription was clear as day as she beaded in on that watch that bore his name before it exploded in a thousand pieces.

She was free, and it felt like she was floating.

The Second Boer War (1899–1902)

Information:

1. Burgers totaled 60291 British Soldiers 458.610 men in arms

2. Total Cost of the war for Britain Pounds 22100000000.

3. Speculation is that the British Commander-in-Chief, Lord Roberts, was influenced by his wife to carry out his "Scorched-Earth-Policy". To revenge the tragic death of his son, lieutenant Freddy Roberts, at the battle of Colenso. Roberts officially sanctions the concentration camp policy by orders to his generals on 14th and 27th September 1900:In doing so he was in contravention and clear breach of Article 42 of the Hague Convention of 1899.

4. "Any person that halves the rations of woman and children. To exert pressure on the family members still in the battle field may just as well have murdered them, the results would have been the same. Innocent woman and children white and black were killed to attain certain political goals "author unknown"

5. Cattle killed fields burnt and over 30000 farms burnt down.

6. Deaths in the camps. Children under 16 22.000 died Women over 16 4.250 Men over 16 1.600 Total deaths 27.900 these are estimated figures

7. 64 camps for blacks were deemed to have existed and operated by the British. Some of these were run in junction with white camps. Mortality rate extreme. Most of deaths occurred amongst children (approx.80 per cent). There are no official figures but it is estimated that at least 14.000 blacks died in British concentration camps. By the end of the war in May 1902 there were still 115.000 blacks being held in custody.

8. Emily Hobouse brought the plight of the Boer woman and children to the British Parliament but was ostracized as being a Boer sympathizer Nothing was done to help.

MAP OF THE BOER REPUBLICS AND CITIES

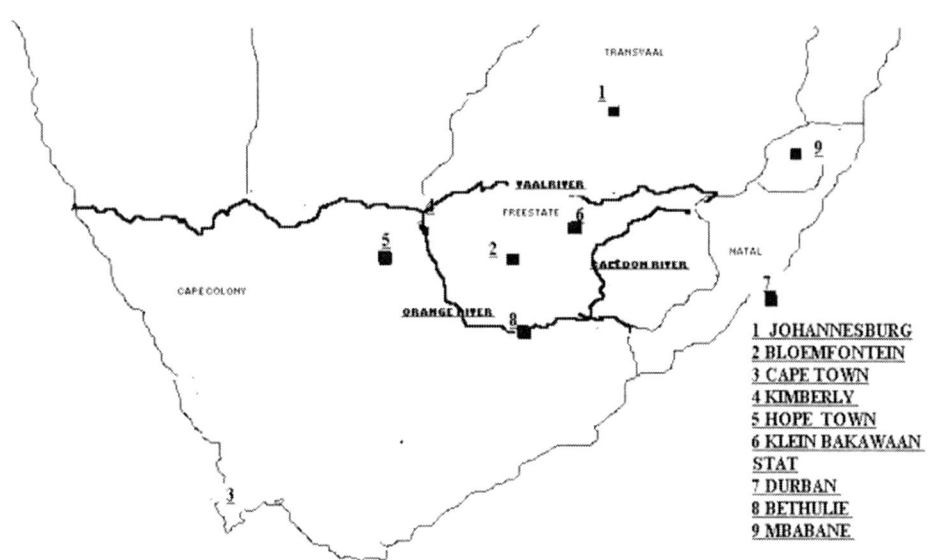

TRANSVAAL

1

9

VAALRIVER

FREESTATE

6

5

2

CALEDON RIVER

NATAL

ORANGE RIVER

8

7

CAPE COLONY

3

1 JOHANNESBURG
2 BLOEMFONTEIN
3 CAPE TOWN
4 KIMBERLY
5 HOPE TOWN
6 KLEIN BAKAWAAN STAT
7 DURBAN
8 BETHULIE
9 MBABANE

CPSIA information can be obtained at www.ICGtesting.com
Printed in the USA
LVOW06s2033270414

383306LV00001BA/17/P